DEATH DANCE

Recent Titles by Geraldine Evans from Severn House

The Rafferty and Llewellyn Mysteries

DYING FOR YOU
ABSOLUTE POISON
BAD BLOOD
LOVE LIES BLEEDING
BLOOD ON THE BONES
A THRUST TO THE VITALS
DEATH DUES
ALL THE LONELY PEOPLE
DEATH DANCE

The Casey and Catt Mysteries

UP IN FLAMES
A KILLING KARMA

Central Support Unit
Catherine Street Dumfries DG1 1JB
tel: 01387 253820   fax: 01387 260294
e-mail: libs&i@dumgal.gov.uk

Dumfries and Galloway
LIBRARIES
Information and Archives

UK

CUSTOMER
SERVICE
EXCELLENCE

24 HOUR LOAN RENEWAL ON OUR WEBSITE - WWW.DUMGAL.GOV.UK/LIA

DEATH DANCE

A Rafferty & Llewellyn Crime Novel

Geraldine Evans

severn
House

This first world edition published 2010
in Great Britain and in the USA by
SEVERN HOUSE PUBLISHERS LTD of
9–15 High Street, Sutton, Surrey, England, SM1 1DF.
Trade paperback edition first published
in Great Britain and the USA 2011 by
SEVERN HOUSE PUBLISHERS LTD.

British Library Cataloguing in Publication Data

Evans, Geraldine.
   Death dance. – (A Rafferty and Llewellyn mystery)
   1. Rafferty, Joseph (Fictitious character)–Fiction.
   2. Llewellyn, Sergeant (Fictitious character)–Fiction.
   3. Police–Great Britain–Fiction. 4. Detective and
   mystery stories.
   I. Title II. Series
   823.9'14-dc22

ISBN-13: 978-0-7278-6937-1   (cased)
ISBN-13: 978-1-84751-274-1   (trade paper)

All Severn House titles are printed on acid-free paper.

Severn House Publishers support The Forest Stewardship Council [FSC],
the leading international forest certification organisation. All our titles that
are printed on Greenpeace-approved FSC-certified paper carry the FSC logo.

Mixed Sources
Product group from well-managed
forests and other controlled sources
www.fsc.org Cert no. SA-COC-1565
© 1996 Forest Stewardship Council
FSC

Typeset by Palimpsest Book Production Ltd.,
Falkirk, Stirlingshire, Scotland.
Printed and bound in Great Britain by
MPG Books Ltd., Bodmin, Cornwall.

ACKNOWLEDGEMENTS

With thanks to my editor, Rachel Simpson Hutchens, for her input. Thanks also to my previous editors, Megan Roberts and Hugo Cox, for keeping my Rafferty & Llewellyn books on track.

DEDICATION

Mollie, this one's for you, with grateful thanks and love for all your thoughtfulness and support.

PROLOGUE

Detective Inspector Joseph Rafferty was only half-listening as Father Kelly led him and his fiancée, Abra, through their wedding rehearsal. The warm sun of an early June evening shining through the stained-glass window was rendering him somnambulistic, and Father Kelly, verbose at the best of times, became even more put-you-to-sleep loquacious on occasions, as today, when he was master of ceremonies, breaking off from the rendition of the service to interject with other bits of information that he thought they needed. Their wedding was three weeks off and things were speeding up, with the days flashing by. It was suddenly becoming all too real and rather scary. Rafferty found himself dwelling more and more on the speech he would have to make on the day. It wasn't something he was looking forward to. He'd made half a dozen attempts at writing a speech and scrapped all of them. His train of thought was briskly interrupted.

'Is it wool-gathering you are, Joseph Rafferty?' Father Kelly demanded in a carrying voice that it was impossible to ignore. 'And amn't I waiting for you to make your responses?'

Rafferty came to with a jerk. 'Sorry, Father. Can you say it again?'

Father Kelly heaved a heavy sigh. 'Sure and it's simple enough. You know your own name, I take it? Say after me – I, Joseph Aloysius—'

'Aloysius?' Beside him at the altar of St Boniface Catholic Church, Abra, his bride-to-be, smothered a giggle. 'I never knew that was your second name.'

'Don't you think I made sure of it?' he retorted. 'I don't know what my mother was thinking of to land me with such a moniker.'

'It's a good saint's name as well as being my father's name,' his ma told him from the second pew. 'And don't be taking my name in vain. I'm right behind you and can hear you.' She put in her two penn'orth about his wandering attention.

'You want to pay heed to Father Kelly when he's talking to you, son. Or I'll never get you married with my grandson on the way.'

'Never mind about that,' Father Kelly admonished. 'Can we get on with it? I've got a Mass to prepare for so I don't want to be coaching you two for the rest of the evening. Now, repeat after me: I, Joseph Aloysius Rafferty take thee, Abra Anne Kearney, to be my lawful wedded wife.'

This time, Rafferty managed to dutifully repeat the words and got through the rest without any further mind wandering.

'So I'll be seeing you at church on Sunday, Joseph?' Father Kelly asked as the rehearsal came to an end.

Rafferty nodded. With the wedding fast approaching, he'd felt obliged to attend Mass. But as a fully-fledged lapsed Catholic he intended to slide out of this obligation at the first opportunity. Father Kelly didn't know this yet, though he probably suspected it. He felt a bit of a hypocrite to be getting married in the Catholic faith, but Father Kelly had more or less taken it for granted and he and his ma had rail-roaded him into it. Abra felt obliged to attend Mass as well, seeing as she was receiving instruction in the faith and had told Father Kelly that she was going to convert to Catholicism. Even Mickey, one of his two younger brothers, had attended today as a stand in for the best man who couldn't attend the rehearsal.

He'd forgotten to turn his mobile off, so he was relieved it didn't go off till the rehearsal was over and he and Abra were back out on the street. He could imagine what Father Kelly would have said if it had gone off in church.

The caller was Sergeant Dafyd Llewellyn, his missing best man. 'I hope I didn't interrupt your wedding rehearsal.'

'No. It's just finished. What's the problem?'

'The body of a woman has been found. It looks like strangulation. A Mrs Adrienne Staveley at a place called The White Farmhouse.'

'Who called it in?'

'Her husband. A Mr John Staveley.'

'OK. Where is it?'

'Off St Mark's Avenue – Lavender Avenue. You can't miss it. I've already called the team out and Dr Dally's on his way.'

'OK. I'll see you there as soon as possible.' Rafferty shut

his mobile and turned to Abra. 'Guess what? Some woman's got herself murdered. I'll have to go.'

'What about me?'

'I'll drop you and Ma home first. I don't know how late I'll be.'

'I suppose this is the shape of things to come.' Abra tossed her long chestnut plait. 'Just don't do a disappearing act after our real wedding ceremony.'

'No chance of that, my sweet.' He kissed her. 'I wouldn't miss our honeymoon for anything.'

'You'd better not. Come on then. Take me and your mum home so you can get off.'

The journey back to the flat didn't take long. His ma told him she'd walk from there to her own home as it was a nice evening. And after kissing them both goodbye, Rafferty quickly drove in the direction of The White Farmhouse. And yet another murder.

ONE

The balmy weather and flower-strewn verges would have made for a pleasant drive out into the country surrounding the Essex market town of Elmhurst, but for what awaited Rafferty at the end of the journey. Another person come to a sudden and violent end. He hated viewing the body of a human being that had presumably been breathing and walking about, enjoying their life and its pleasures such a short time before being brutally murdered.

He wondered what the world would be like without him in it. He found it difficult to imagine himself not existing. But the world had gone on for countless millennia before he was born and would doubtless continue after his death, strange as he might find the fact. 'Joe Rafferty centre of the universe,' he murmured to the empty car. 'Not.'

After he'd passed a sizeable house and driven on a further hundred yards down Lavender Avenue, it wasn't difficult to realize he had arrived at the right place with all the police vehicles and flashing lights to point the way. Perversely, the White Farmhouse was painted yellow. It stood in spacious grounds and had several outbuildings. The green front door stood wide open. Rafferty said hello to the young PC Timothy Smales, looking important with his clipboard. He climbed into his protective gear and ducked under the police tape.

'Dr Dally here yet?' he asked.

'Just arrived, sir,' Smales informed him as he entered Rafferty's name on his clipboard in his best, schoolboy handwriting.

Rafferty nodded acknowledgement.

The scene of crime team had yet to arrive so the farmhouse was peaceful. The house was quite substantial, Rafferty noted as he paused in the doorway to get his bearings. There was a wide hallway leading from the front of the house right through to the rear, with two doors opening on either side and stairs to the left. He slowly paced his way to the first two doors. There was a large room with a desk and a computer off to the left, with the even more spacious drawing room off to the right. Llewellyn was in there with a man Rafferty guessed was the husband. He entered and Llewellyn stood up and introduced them.

Rafferty acknowledged John Staveley with a nod, but he wasn't ready to question him yet and he gestured for Llewellyn to come into the hall and bring him up to date.

'So, what's occurring?' he asked after Llewellyn left the drawing room and shut the door behind him.

'I've just been speaking to John Staveley, the victim's husband.'

'And what does he have to say for himself?'

'That he was out all day. Came home around six and found his wife dead in the kitchen.'

'Anyone with him when he found her?'

'No one.'

'Anyone else live in the house?'

'Kyle, Mr Staveley's son by a previous marriage. He's a schoolboy. He's out, but according to his father he's expected back any time.'

'How old is he?'

'Sixteen.'

Rafferty nodded and muttered, 'Teenage angst. Better have a look at the body. In the kitchen you said?'

'Yes. It's next door on the left. The dining room's opposite.'

When they entered the large, modern and expensively outfitted kitchen Dr Dally was busy about his usual examination and didn't welcome the interruption. 'Last to arrive as usual, Rafferty,' he said irascibly as he eased his plump knees on the hard stone floor.

'I was at my wedding rehearsal when Dafyd phoned,' he defended himself against this unjust accusation. 'Anyway, you're a fine one to talk. You're not known as Dilly Dally for nothing.' Rafferty nodded at the woman's corpse. The body was on its back with the legs bent. There was purple bruising to the throat and the face and neck were dark red and congested and looked even more so when adjoined by a white sleeveless top. 'Any idea how long she's been dead?'

'No more than an hour and a half. Two hours, tops.

Strangled, as you can see. Done manually. He left the marks of his fingers on the skin.'

'There were no signs of a break-in at the front,' Rafferty said. 'What about at the back?' he asked Llewellyn.

'No. Nothing like that. Either she let her killer in or they were here already.'

'The husband, you mean. I'll have a word with him now. See if he feels like incriminating himself.'

This remark was on the receiving end of a pained expression from the Welshman. You've only just got here, it seemed to say, and haven't even spoken to the man yet, but you're ready to place him in the role of chief suspect.

They walked back along the hallway and into the drawing room. John Staveley was still sitting as before, with his hands clenched between his knees and his head bowed, seemingly unaware of their entrance.

'Mr Staveley,' Rafferty began, to get his attention.

Slowly, John Staveley looked up, blinking. He brushed his straight dark hair out of his eyes with long, slim fingers. His deathly pallor, combined with his black hair and thin face, gave him a Draculaesque appearance. Rafferty, half-expecting him to bare his teeth in a snarl, found his hand reaching for his throat in a protective gesture. Sheepishly, as he became aware of what he was doing and why, he dropped his hand back to his side.

Rafferty introduced himself. 'I'm sorry to have to speak to you at such a time, sir, but there are a few questions I need to ask. Was your wife expecting any visitors this afternoon or evening?' Rafferty sat on the settee opposite. Llewellyn did the same and got his notebook out again.

'Not that I know of, but she is – was – a sociable woman. People would drop in to see her without ringing first.'

'Did she have a job?' Rafferty was thinking about work colleagues he could question about the dead woman and was disappointed to learn that this wasn't an option.

'No. Until I was made redundant six months ago I earned enough to keep all of us.'

'You were made redundant? The last months must have been difficult for you.'

'Yes. You could say that.'

'You haven't been able to find another job?'

'No.' This last was said with a note of bitterness. 'It's not for want of trying. I go to the Job Centre every day.'

'What time did you go there today?'

'My normal time. Nine o'clock.'

'I understand you were out all day. Where did you go after the Job Centre?'

'I stayed in town. I took a newspaper to the public library to study the job vacancies.'

'What's your line of work?'

'I'm an engineer. Or I was. Now all the Job Centre can offer me is factory work or shelf-stacking.' The bitter note was back. Staveley had rather beautiful brown eyes. They were large, with clear whites and long lashes. At the moment, unsurprisingly, his gaze was troubled and his lashes shielded his eyes as if he preferred to avoid meeting another's gaze. Especially Rafferty's.

'You told my sergeant you didn't get back home till six o'clock this evening.'

'That's right. That's when I found my wife lying dead on the kitchen floor.'

'So you were out all day. What were you doing, apart from going to the Job Centre and the library?'

'I just walked around. Had a couple in the pub. Nothing much.'

'You must have spent several hours just walking around. Pretty tiring.'

'I'm all right. I'm used to it. I do it most days.'

Which, to Rafferty, pointed to a reluctance to go home. Why? Hadn't he and his wife got on? There was no time like the present to find out. 'Were you and your wife happy together, Mr Staveley?'

'What's this? The husband as the guilty party?' Strangely, the possibility didn't seem to worry him. 'I thought we were happy. Happy enough, anyway. But since I was made redundant I've been getting on her nerves. Under her feet all day. That's why I stay out. It gives – gave – us both some space. The lack of money doesn't help either. Adrienne was used to me earning good money. She was used to spending it, too. We've both had to pull our horns in. I've had to take my son, Kyle, out of private school. He's at the local comprehensive now. He hates it. I know he's desperately unhappy there, but there's nothing I can do about it.' He swept the black hair off his forehead in a gesture of despair.

Just then, there was a commotion at the front door.

'Let me in. I live here. Dad! Dad!' A gangly six-foot youth almost fell into the drawing room, a flustered Timothy Smales close behind him. 'What's happened?'

'Kyle. You're home. Where have you been till this time?'

'Nowhere. Tell me what's happened.'

Rafferty gestured for Smales to return to the front of the house.

'It's your stepmother. She's dead. Murdered.'

'I didn't do it,' Kyle blurted out.

That he should immediately think to deny any involvement rather than ask how she had died brought a stunned silence. His father quickly broke into the silence to say, 'No one thinks you did.'

Kyle didn't look too sure that this was so. His face was flushed and he fumbled awkwardly at his pockets as if trying to hide hands that suddenly seemed too large and guilt-clumsy.

Rafferty butted in. 'I take it you didn't get on with your stepmother, Kyle?'

'Not really. I tried to stay out of the house most of the time. She always made me feel I was in the way. She wanted me to go to boarding school, but Dad wouldn't hear of it. I'd have gone like a shot, but there's no chance of that with money so tight.'

'And no need with your stepmother dead,' Rafferty pointed out.

'No, I suppose not.'

There was another awkward silence, then Rafferty stood up. 'I'll need to have one of my officers take the fingerprints of both of you – just for the purposes of elimination. If you'll wait here.'

He called Fraser, the dabs man, in. The fingerprints were quickly taken and Rafferty said, 'I'll want to talk to both of you again. The kitchen's going to be out of bounds for a day or two – is there anywhere you can go in the meantime?'

'I suppose we could go to my mother's,' said Staveley as he stood up. 'She doesn't live far and she's got plenty of spare bedrooms.'

'If you can let me have the address.'

Staveley did so and Llewellyn made a note of it.

'Perhaps you'd like to pack a bag and I'll get one of my officers to drive you there.'

'There's no need. I can drive.' Staveley turned to his son. 'Come on, Kyle, you can put a few things together, too. Not too much.' He glanced at Rafferty. 'I presume we won't be away from home for long.' He nodded to Llewellyn and went out, closely followed by his son. Rafferty heard the thump of footsteps on the stairs. Ten minutes later they were back, John Staveley with car keys in one hand and a leather holdall in the other.

'I'd better ring my mother,' he said. 'Let her know what's happened and that she'll have to put us up for a day or two.' He dropped his holdall, pulled a mobile from his jacket pocket, jabbed at a few keys and had a low, murmured conversation, then he and Kyle left.

Rafferty and Llewellyn went back to the kitchen. Dr Sam Dally was just finishing up. The SOCOs were busy dusting surfaces and sweeping dust and other particles from the floor.

'Where's the nearest neighbour?' he asked Llewellyn.

'About one hundred yards nearer the main road.' Llewellyn was well aware of Rafferty's dislike of the use of metric measurements and always used imperial. 'That and the Staveley's place are the only houses in the road as it finishes in a dead end another fifty yards further along.'

Rafferty remembered passing another house at the beginning of Lavender Avenue, the side road leading to the Farmhouse. 'Better send someone to check if they saw anything or heard any cars.'

Llewellyn nodded and went out.

Rafferty returned to the empty drawing room and sat down to think through what to do next. Kyle and John Staveley would have to be questioned more thoroughly as to their whereabouts this afternoon and early evening. The son was as tall as his father and had admitted he hadn't got on with his stepmother. He looked strong enough to manually strangle the slender Adrienne and there was certainly no love lost there.

And then there was John Staveley. Money worries inevitably brought tension. It had apparently developed to such an extent that Staveley had taken to staying out all day. He would need to talk to Staveley's mother and see what he could learn from her about their relationship. The neighbours, too, might be able to tell them something about the Staveley household.

He had obtained the address of Staveley's mother so he could speak to her at any time. There would also be friends and possibly other relatives they could talk to.

He went back to the kitchen. The coroner's officer had just given permission for the body to be removed. Sam Dally was still there, chatting to Adrian Appleby, head of the SOCOs.

'All done, Doc?' Rafferty asked.

'For now. I doubt I'll be able to tell you more than I already have even after I get her on the table.' He began to pack his instruments back in his bag.

Rafferty nodded. He hadn't expected any more: it looked a simple enough murder with little in the way of complications from the pathologist's point of view.

The SOCOs would be here for some time, but there was no need for him to be. He would go back to the station and write up his report. But before he could make good this intention, Llewellyn and the officer he had despatched to the neighbours returned with the news that the victim had regularly entertained a male visitor when her husband was out.

'Chap called Gary Oldfield,' Llewellyn told him. 'The neighbour said she often saw his car parked outside when she took her dogs for a walk.'

'Just good friends or rather more?' Rafferty mused. 'Does she know where this Oldfield lives?'

'No. But she knows where he works. That second-hand car lot on Station Road. He's a used car salesman.'

Rafferty grinned. 'Bit of a cliché if he was her lover. I wonder if the husband was aware of these visits.'

'What is it they say?' Llewellyn intoned. 'That the husband is usually the last one to find out.'

'Not always. And maybe not in this case.'

TWO

The victim's friend, Gary Oldfield, when they spoke to him the following morning, was full of surface charm and what he obviously thought was a winning line in patter. He was in his late twenties and had a mass of curly dark brown hair of which he was clearly immensely proud. He kept running his fingers through it as though to reassure himself that it was still there. And while such a gesture might draw attention to his hair, it also brought attention to his fingernails, which were badly bitten and at odds with his otherwise smart appearance. Altogether, with his sharp suit, his hair, his ingratiating manner and his too-ready smile, he didn't find favour with Rafferty. In this way, he matched the cars for sale.

The used car lot was the usual collection of dubious bargains. But they all gleamed proudly in the sunshine as if at heart they were Rolls Royces. The lot occupied roughly a half-acre plot on Station Road, situated between the Railway Arms and a charity shop. The site office consisted of a Portakabin. Gary Oldfield leant carelessly against the office desk while they questioned him. He professed himself shocked at Adrienne Staveley's murder and, as though to prove it, he ran his hand through his hair again and shook his head.

'I gather you were a regular visitor to the Farmhouse,' said Rafferty. 'You and Adrienne Staveley must have been good friends.'

Oldfield took a few seconds to answer as though debating with himself how much he should admit to. Finally, he said, 'We were. I'm gutted that she's dead.'

'How did you meet?'

'At the local tennis club. She was always great fun, the real life and soul. I'll miss her.'

The tennis club seemed an unlikely place for the used car salesman to frequent; maybe he went there to pull the ladies. Certainly the female of the species was likely to be found there in some numbers, presumably from a desire similar to Oldfield's.

'What did her husband think of your visiting her? I gather it was invariably when he was out that you called round.'

Oldfield shrugged and gave another winning smile. It did nothing for Rafferty. 'I never saw him, so I don't know what he thought. You'd have to ask him. As for me calling round when he was out, that's just the way it happened. It was Adrienne I wanted to see, not the rest of the family. I found her stepson a surly youth and he was mostly in during the evenings. Adrienne and I would have a few drinks and a few laughs. I'd often drop round during my lunch break and Adrienne would make me a sandwich.' He moved to sit behind the desk as though he thought it prudent to put the width of a metal barrier between them.

'Where were you, Mr Oldfield, between four and six yesterday evening?'

'Why? Do you want to put me in the frame for Adrienne's murder?' He grinned as if he found this possibility worthy of merriment. I'm a personable young man, the grin seemed to say. How can you possibly suspect me? 'As it happens, I was at home from four o'clock onwards. I was there all evening. With my girlfriend. You can check with her, if you like.'

'Thank you. I will,' Rafferty told him. 'What's her name and where's home?'

'She's called Diana Rexton. We've got a flat around the corner in Abbot's Walk. No 18A.'

'And is she likely to be there this evening if we call round about eight o'clock?'

'Yes. Di's a homebody. She rarely even wants to go to the tennis club since she met me.'

She'd landed her man so there was no need, thought Rafferty. Poor bitch. He thought she should get herself back there smartish and land herself another one.

'Do you always finish work so early?'

'No. But I often work odd hours and the boss gives me time off in lieu.'

For the fourth time since they'd entered the Portakabin Gary Oldfield ran his fingers through his hair. Rafferty caught a glimpse of what looked like an expensive watch. It was a slim, sleek gold.

He was beginning to wonder whether the hand-running-through-the-hair routine was a nervous action rather than one caused by vanity. 'Tell me, Mr Oldfield, were you and Mrs Staveley a bit more than friends?'

Oldfield gave a lazy smile, linked his hands behind his head and leaned back in his chair as if to demonstrate how relaxed he was at this line of questioning.

'I wish. No. We were no more than friends. The last six months hadn't been a happy time for Adrienne. I guess I provided her with a bit of light relief after her husband was made redundant. She was bored and liked male company, that's all. It's why she joined the tennis club. I'd often see her there when I wasn't working in the afternoons. She had a mean backhand. She complained that her old man had become very morose since he lost his job. They barely talked and when they did they rowed.'

Was Oldfield trying to throw suspicion on John Staveley? Or was he simply telling the truth? Of course, it could always be a mix of the two, but if it was the former the question that occurred to Rafferty was why Oldfield should want to thrust suspicion on Staveley? Was his own alibi somewhat shaky? Wasn't he sure his girlfriend would back him up or that she wouldn't lie convincingly if she did?

Beneath the too-charming exterior Rafferty thought Oldfield would probably be a nasty piece of work if anyone crossed him. He suspected he was getting a kick out of stirring things up. The running of the fingers through his hair was beginning to get on his nerves.

'We may need to speak to you again, sir,' Rafferty told him as he made for the door.

'I'm always available, Inspector.' The smile flashed again. 'If I'm not here, I'll likely be at home. We don't go out much Diana and me.'

They left it there and drove to John Staveley's mother's house to find out what they could. She lived in the village of Elmwood to the south east of Elmhurst. It wasn't a long drive. The house was modern, detached and double-fronted, with white painted walls and a glossy black door. The property had a good-sized front garden, surfaced with zigzagged brick, which provided room to park as many as six cars. It was screened from the road by high privet hedges.

A woman that Rafferty took to be Mrs Staveley Senior answered the door. She looked a formidable woman with sharp ice-blue eyes and iron-grey hair worn in a severe cut. Although she must have been in her sixties, she had retained her figure and she looked very trim in a grey trouser suit. She held herself ramrod straight and such was her posture, she could have been an officer just graduated from Sandhurst.

'Yes?'

'Mrs Staveley, we're police officers. We'd like to speak to your son and grandson.'

The icy blue gaze sharpened even more. 'I thought you'd already spoken to them. They're both in mourning and should be left to their grief. I don't know what else you think they can tell you.'

'Neither do I until I speak to them.'

She met his gaze with another challenging stare, which she held for several seconds. Then she seemed to accept that Rafferty had the upper hand and stood back. 'You'd better come in.' She shut the door behind them. 'Follow me.'

She led them along a wide and bare white-painted hallway into a large drawing room with no frills. Upright black armchairs were matched by a similarly upright settee. The pictures on the walls were stark black and white abstracts. There were no plants or flowers and no ornaments. Even the family photographs were few in number and grouped neatly on a bureau. The carpet was a plain institutionalized mid-grey.

The only aspects that softened the room were the sprawled figures of John and Kyle Staveley, They made the army-neat room seem untidy. The two looked very alike as they sat side by side: same wiry frames, black hair, clear brown eyes and pale skin. Rafferty surmised that they must take after Staveley's father. Mrs Staveley Senior invited them to sit down and did so herself.

'Mr Staveley, Kyle, I've come to ask a few more questions.' Rafferty was conscious of Mrs Staveley watching him as she sat as bolt upright as her chair. Rafferty did his best to ignore her intimidating stare as he sat down. 'Kyle, I didn't ask you before, but can you tell me where you were yesterday between four and six o'clock?'

'I was at the library, studying.' Kyle's large, bony hands clutched one another as if seeking reassurance.

Rafferty tried to put the clearly uncomfortable youth at his ease. 'At the library? I thought all youngsters nowadays did their studying on the internet. I presume you've got your own computer?'

'Of course. But not all of us go in for the slavish copying that the comprehensive students think good enough. I like to do original work.' There was the contempt of the scholar in his voice as he dismissed the study habits of his peers.

'Very commendable.' Rafferty doubted that such an attitude made him popular at school and he wondered if Kyle was bullied. He turned to John Staveley. 'I gather that your wife was in the habit of regularly entertaining a male visitor while you were out. Were you aware of this?'

'No.' Staveley sounded defensive, which, in the circumstances, wasn't altogether surprising. 'Why would I be? I never saw him.'

'His name's Gary Oldfield. Did you know him at all? Have you heard of him?'

'No. I know nothing about him.' John Staveley's lips formed a thin line. 'Why are you asking me all these questions?'

'Your wife's been murdered, sir, that's why. Are you sure you didn't know Oldfield?'

'My son has told you he knows nothing about this man, Inspector,' Mrs Staveley interrupted. 'Why must you continue to badger him?' The iron-grey hair seemed to bristle as she sat forward and challenged him.

'Because his wife is dead, Mrs Staveley. Murdered, as I said. I need to get to the bottom of it.' Rafferty met her gaze. He refused to be intimidated by her.

'My son had nothing to do with it. Neither did my grandson. They were both out during the times you mention, when presumably Adrienne was killed. My son only got back home at six o'clock, which is when he found her.'

'Yet I understand he and his wife hadn't been getting on. It's natural to ask him about any male friends his wife had and whether he knew about them.'

'He's already told you he didn't. He spends very little time at home. Even in the evenings, when he is there, he tends to shut himself up in his study with his computer, looking for work. If dedication to a task meant anything he'd have found a worthwhile job by now. It's been a very difficult time for him.

If that wife of his had been any good, she'd have looked for a job herself and helped to pay the bills.'

'I take it you didn't like your son's wife?'

'I neither liked her nor disliked her. She was my son's wife and as such I accepted her.' As though determined not to betray any anxiety at this line of questioning, her hands rested lightly on either side of her chair. She looked the very epitome of a woman taking her ease.

It seemed none of her husband's family had liked Adrienne. 'Did Mrs Staveley Junior have any close relatives? Parents or siblings? I should have asked you this yesterday,' Rafferty confessed as he turned back to John Staveley.

'No. Her parents are dead and she was an only child,' Staveley told them.

That was something, thought Rafferty. No bad news to break. Llewellyn would be relieved, as he had, ever since his Methodist minister father had made him accompany him to break news of a death, always fought shy of such deeds.

'Have you any other family I can ask about your wife's friends – someone she might have confided in?'

'There's my sister and her husband. Helen and David Ayling,' Staveley told him. 'Though I can't see Adrienne confiding in either of them. They weren't close.'

Rafferty asked them for the Aylings' address and Llewellyn noted it down.

'What about women friends?'

Mrs Staveley gave an unladylike snort. 'She wasn't one for women friends. I can't think of one. What about you, John?'

Her son shook his head. 'I can't think of anyone either, though she did sometimes chat with Sarah Jones, the wife of our nearest neighbour. I don't think their conversation went much beyond trivial things like the weather, but she did sometimes come over for coffee on a Sunday morning.'

'I see. Well that's all for now.' Rafferty got up from the unyielding settee, glad to relieve his backside: it had been getting numb. 'Thank you for your time. We'll see ourselves out.'

'On the contrary,' said Mrs Staveley. '*I'll* see you out.' She got up from her chair with a determined air.

Rafferty stifled a grin. Clearly she wanted to make sure they left rather than lingered in the hall to eavesdrop.

'She's a bit of a tartar,' he said to Llewellyn when they were back in the car. He gazed through the windscreen as rain lashed it. The weather was changeable. It had been dry when they had entered Mrs Staveley's home. He prayed it didn't rain on his and Abra's wedding day.

'I suppose she sees that you suspect her son,' Llewellyn commented. 'She was certainly very protective of him. Natural enough in the circumstances.'

'I suppose so. I'm surprised Staveley didn't ask when he and his son could go back home. His mother's doesn't look the most comfortable of places. I bet the beds are as rigid as the settee.'

'I don't imagine they relish the prospect of returning home after what happened there.' Llewellyn did up his seatbelt and put the key in the ignition preparatory to driving off.

'No. I don't suppose they do,' said Rafferty as he did up his own seatbelt. 'Let's get over and see Staveley's sister. Though as she and the victim weren't close I don't hold out much hope of learning anything useful.'

Helen and David Ayling lived in the small and ancient hamlet of St Botolph to the south of Elmhurst. It didn't take long to drive there from Mrs Staveley's. It was a house somewhat smaller than Mrs Staveley Senior's home, but it was still substantial. It was thatched and picture-postcard pretty – Rafferty could imagine Americans lining up to photograph it when the summer tourist season got into full swing.

David Ayling was at work, but his wife was at home. Although a large woman, of around forty, Helen Ayling looked stylish in a smart pair of black trousers and a thin, tan cowl-neck jumper. She had a look of Staveley, sharing her brother's black hair, dark eyes and pale skin, though her hair looked as if it had a bit of assistance from the dye bottle. She seemed very much the protective older sister. She invited them into her home, and when they were all seated around the inglenook fireplace in a living room as large and stylish as its owner, with two cream settees and an oak dresser that, with its silvery-grey wood, looked very old, she asked them how the case was going.

'Slowly as yet,' Rafferty replied. 'But it's early days as your sister-in-law was only killed yesterday. I wonder what you can tell me about her. Do you know any of her friends, for instance? Anyone who could shed some light on her character.'

Helen Ayling gave a short laugh. 'I can do that all right. Although I don't like to speak ill of the dead, Adrienne was a woman who liked a good time. She was happy enough when the money was coming in, but once my brother was made redundant and the money dried up, she became very dissatisfied. I suggested she get a job, but she just laughed at me as if she thought the idea was ludicrous. You'd think she'd want to help, but not a bit of it. She wasn't the sort of wife who was a helpmeet.'

Clearly, Helen Ayling hadn't approved of her sister-in-law any more than had her mother.

'What about her friends? Did you know any of them?'

'I know she had men friends, several of them. I occasionally saw her with one or the other in town having lunch. I don't know any women friends.'

'Do you know the names and addresses of these men friends?'

'As it happens, I do – not their addresses, but their names. One's called Gary Oldfield. The other's called Michael Peacock.'

'Do you think there was more between them and Adrienne than just friendship?'

'I wouldn't be surprised. Adrienne was a terrible flirt. It used to upset my brother, but she wouldn't stop. I sometimes think she did it just to spite him. She could be a difficult, headstrong woman.' She paused, then asked, 'Do you think one of these men killed her?'

'As to that, we don't know.' He didn't add that John Staveley was inevitably a suspect as the husband of the victim. But Helen Ayling seemed to be an intelligent woman and even if she chose not to bring it up, she must be aware of the possibility of her brother's guilt, particularly as, by his own admission, he and his wife hadn't been getting along. As the protective older sister, she would surely have known of the situation as regards their marriage.

'Tell me, Mrs Ayling, were you at home between four and six yesterday evening?'

'Why? Am I a suspect?'

'We're just trying to eliminate as many people as possible.'

'As it happens, I was at home. My husband didn't get back from work till around six thirty.'

'I see. Thank you. That's all for now, but we may need to question you again.' He told her they would need to take her fingerprints and if she could come into the station for this procedure it would be helpful. Rafferty thanked her again and they got in the car and returned to the station.

Superintendent Bradley had left a message with Bill Beard on reception that he wanted to see Rafferty as soon as he returned.

'What sort of mood is he in?' he questioned Bill. 'Am I going to get my head bitten off?'

'It's a bit early in the case even for him to go off on one,' said Bill. 'But he wants to see you straight away, so I'd get along there smartish.'

Rafferty pulled a face and headed for Bradley's first floor office.

Bradley didn't beat about the bush. 'So what's happening?' he asked as soon as Rafferty had knocked and entered.

'We've interviewed nearly everyone with a connection to the dead woman. She almost certainly had a lover if not more than one. One is probably a Gary Oldfield. And as she hadn't been getting on with her husband, he's also a strong suspect.'

'Any evidence?'

'Not yet. But he doesn't have an alibi. He told us he was out just wandering the streets when Adrienne died.'

'Sounds an unlikely alibi. Didn't you say there's a stepson as well?'

'Yes. Kyle. He's sixteen and he didn't get on with the dead woman either. In fact none of her husband's family seem to have liked her very much, including her mother-in-law and sister-in-law.'

'So she was an unpopular woman with the females in the family. Strangulation though. That's generally a man's crime. Anyway, get your report written up and let me have it as soon as possible.'

'Yes, sir.' Rafferty exited the super's office smartly. The old man had been in a benign mood for a change. It was a welcome relief from the usual sarcasm. He went back to his office and wrote up his report as the super had instructed.

That job done, he sat back and stared into space before he said to Llewellyn, 'So what do you think, Daff? Did the husband do it?'

'It sounds as if he had cause.'

'Mmm. The way she entertained that Gary Oldfield regularly in her home doesn't suggest innocence to me. I can't believe John Staveley wasn't aware of it.'

'He doesn't have a credible alibi, either.'

'What about the mother-in-law? She seemed formidable enough to be prepared to commit murder, especially for her precious son's sake.'

'Yes, but strangulation. It's not a woman's crime.'

'That's what the super said.'

'And he's right.'

'Still, it's possible.' For once, Rafferty was determined to keep an open mind. It wasn't his usual practice. No wonder Llewellyn looked surprised.

The post-mortem was scheduled for after lunch, so Rafferty and Llewellyn drove over to Elmhurst General Hospital where the mortuary was situated. They were the last to arrive. They joined the coroner's officer, the scene of crime officer and the photographer and video operator round the steel table.

Dr Sam Dally greeted them and asked acerbically, 'So, it's all right if I make a start now, is it Inspector Rafferty?'

'No need to be sarcastic, Sam. We're not late – or not much. We're ready when you are.'

'Right.' Sam turned to the microphone suspended over the table and gave the cadaver's details: name, age and special characteristics. He described the body, commenting on every abnormality. His assistant took Adrienne Staveley's fingerprints after taking scrapings from under her nails in case she'd managed to claw her attacker during the assault on her. After he had taken various bodily samples, Sam Dally opened her up in the classic 'Y' formation. Once he had removed, and had his assistant weigh, the internal organs, he gave his attention to the neck, taking a sample of the bruised flesh.

'The larynx and hyoid bone are fractured,' he intoned into the microphone, 'so the victim was definitely strangled. By the position of the bruises, the assault was a frontal one and manual rather than by means of a ligature.'

The PM continued for another fifteen minutes, then Sam pulled off his gloves, threw them in the general direction of the waste bin and gestured to his assistant that he could sew the victim up.

Fortunately, the body had been found quickly. Sometimes a cadaver was in such a bad way that Rafferty had to resort to breathing through his mouth and holding his nose. Still, even though the body was in a fresh condition, Rafferty had elected to postpone lunch until the PM was over – the awful offaliness of the procedure tended to make him feel sick to his stomach – something he had learned during previous procedures. Llewellyn, of course, as if to make Rafferty appear even more squeamish, was unaffected by the smells, sights and sounds of a PM.

Sam whipped off his protective gown, turned to Rafferty, and observed, 'Not long now till the big day. How's Abra bearing up at the thought of becoming Mrs Rafferty? Not getting cold feet?'

'Of course she's not getting cold feet. Why would she?' Why did everyone keep asking him that? Rafferty wondered irritably. And why did no one ask if *he* was getting frosty extremities?

'Not every woman considers that marrying a policeman is the best they can do. In fact, I would think that Abra could certainly do far better and find herself a man who earned more, worked fewer hours and didn't keep letting her down over social arrangements. Perhaps she'll realize that before the wedding.'

That was something Rafferty worried about a lot. Stung, even though he knew Sam was joking, he retorted, 'I imagine your lady friend thinks the same about you. It can't be nice to contemplate what the hands of a man in such a job do all day before he comes home to her.'

Rafferty felt a bit mean-spirited after he'd said it. Because Sam's wife had died a year or so ago and for a time he'd been morose and inclined to be snappy. But then he'd met Mary, a lady of his own age and he was nowadays a far more contented soul.

Sam smiled and told him, 'My lady's not squeamish like you, Rafferty. Stomach of iron she's got. In fact she's so not discombobulated by my job that she's come in more than once

and watched me perform PMs. Nor does she forego her lunch
before doing so, unlike some people I could mention.'

Rafferty pulled a face at this below-the-belt riposte and said
to Llewellyn, 'Come on. Let's get out of here. I've heard
enough for one day about both my wussy stomach and my
unworthiness as a bridegroom.' He walked to the door,
followed by Llewellyn. Sam's derisive laughter floated after
them.

They went back to the station and yet more paperwork.
They worked steadily through it. Finally, Rafferty slumped
back in his chair, glanced at the clock and said, 'Time's getting
on, Dafyd. Let's get ourselves over to Gary Oldfield's place
and see if his girlfriend can confirm his alibi.'

But Oldfield was alone when they got to his flat, with no
alibi-confirming girlfriend in sight.

'So where is your girlfriend, Mr Oldfield? Rafferty asked.
'You said if we came over this evening she would be here.'

'I thought she would be, but she decided to go to her parents
for a few days.'

'Well, we need to speak to her, so can you let me have
their address?'

Oldfield rattled it off and Llewellyn noted it down.

Rafferty's interest pricked up at once when he heard the
name. 'Heathcote Manor? Sounds an interesting place.'

Rafferty came from a long line of builders and house reno-
vators. His brothers were both in the trade as were most of
his cousins. Mickey was a carpenter and Patrick Sean was a
brickie. Rafferty and his cousin, Nigel, were the only ones
who had gone off in a different direction. Rafferty, pushed by
his mother, into the police and Nigel, because he had both a
love of money and a horror of getting honest dirt on his hands,
had gone into the estate agency business.

'Yeah,' said Oldfield. 'Worth a fortune. It's Elizabethan. Or
something. Cold and draughty, anyway. Give me a modern
house any day.'

This was sacrilege as far as Rafferty was concerned. He
had, over the years, developed a love of old buildings; it had
turned him into something of a history buff.

According to Oldfield, Heathcote Manor was in the country
to the northeast of Elmhurst, not that far from the ruined priory
that Henry VIII had destroyed during the dissolution.

He thought it odd that Diana Rexton should have found it necessary to stay overnight with her parents when she lived in the same town. He suspected she and Oldfield had had a row and he wondered what about. Had Oldfield asked her to lie for him about where he'd been when Adrienne Staveley was murdered?

THREE

But Oldfield wasn't saying, so they left him to his poky modern flat in a nondescript block in the poorer part of the town and drove to Diana Rexton's parents' place. It was a gloriously warm and bright evening, which made for a pleasant run out and, for once, Rafferty was happy for Llewellyn to do the driving. He sat back and enjoyed the journey and didn't urge Llewellyn to get a move on, as he usually did.

The house, when they found it, down one of the quiet lanes leading eventually to the A12, was an exquisite Elizabethan gem, with tall chimneys and rose-red brick softened and weathered by the centuries. The huge window of the great hall was still in place and it looked like it was the original – as he got nearer, he could see the wavy glass that had been used in the sixteenth century.

He became conscious that his heart was beating a little faster and that his mouth had gone dry. He couldn't wait to see inside – he so hoped it hadn't been ruined by some 'improving' Victorian gentleman as so many had.

He wasn't disappointed. Once the massive oak door had been opened – by a middle-aged man in a threadbare cardigan and baggy corduroy trousers, whom Rafferty presumed was the odd-job man – and he had explained his business, he was led inside and saw that it had scarcely been touched by the passing of the centuries. It really was an architectural marvel and Rafferty felt a pang of envy for its owner. How he'd love to live in such a place. Oldfield must be a barbarian indeed if the first thought he had about the house was in terms of its financial rather than its architectural and historical value. 'Cold and draughty' was how he had described it. Rafferty would willingly put up with any number of draughts to live in such a house and enjoy the rich texture of history all around him.

By the time the odd-job man had gone in search of Diana Rexton, Rafferty had almost forgotten the purpose of his visit, so lost was he in soaking up the atmosphere of the great hall, with its mighty oak beams and the enormous window that flooded the huge space with light. There was a mass of photographs scattered about the room: on the windowsills, the manorial-sized mantelpiece, on the walls amongst the ancestor portraits that, judging from the clothing worn by the subjects, went back to when the house was built. An outstandingly pretty girl featured in the vast majority of them. Diana Rexton, he presumed. She had dark shining curls and delicate skin. The fireplace was currently playing host to a massive display of dried flowers. It was very well done and Rafferty wondered who had created it as it had a professional air to it. He could imagine the fireplace on a cold winter night, its flames crackling among the logs as the family sat around the fire telling each other ghost stories. He wondered if they had a resident ghost. It seemed that kind of place. He wondered if—

He forced himself back to the present with an effort of will when somebody said his name. It was a wrench.

'I'm Diana Rexton, Inspector. What can I do for you?'

Rafferty did a double take when he saw her. For this wasn't the gorgeous girl in all the photographs. *This* Diana Rexton was plain, with a pallid slab of a face. She had bad skin and looked dowdy in well-worn jodhpurs and a jumper that was a match for the odd-job man's holey cardigan. Her body looked wiry rather than slender, and he would bet that under her clothes she was well muscled. How she could have brought herself to believe that the shallow Gary Oldfield could possibly be interested in her for anything other than her money . . .

'Miss Rexton,' he said. 'I'm here about the murder of a Mrs Adrienne Staveley. I understand your boyfriend knew her quite well.' 'Knew' in the biblical sense, he felt like adding, if only to save her from Gary Oldfield's greedy clutches. Because it was clear that her money was what Oldfield was after. The family must be loaded to live in such a house. Rafferty could imagine the sort of woman that would really appeal to Oldfield: blondes, probably of the bottled variety, who wore short, short skirts and tops low-slung enough to show off their considerable assets.

'Yes,' she replied. 'My father said. How can I help you, Inspector?'

'I just need to ask you a few questions. Nothing to worry about.' Rafferty was surprised to learn that the 'odd-job' man was her father and presumably the seriously rich owner of the house. He was surprised, too, that her father hadn't stayed to give her moral support once he knew what Rafferty wanted to see his daughter about.

She had straw in her straggly mousy hair and when Rafferty pointed this out to her, she ran her hand through her hair till she found it and removed it. She crushed it and dropped it in the huge fireplace. Her wry smile transformed her face and showed how attractive she could have been had nature been kinder to her.

'Sorry,' she said. 'I've been with Benjy.'

'Benjy?' Rafferty repeated, imagining that she'd been rolling in the hay with some country bumpkin who couldn't afford to take her to a hotel. He wondered did Oldfield know he wasn't the only one who had been playing away.

Then she explained and Rafferty knew his imagination had led him astray. Not for the first time.

'Benjy's my horse. Sixteen hands of muscle with a temper.' She laughed, showing off well-tended, middle-class teeth. 'If I forget to bring him an apple or carrot in the morning when I muck him out, he tries to kick me. He broke my wrist last year. Evil brute.' She turned and picked up one of the photographs that was on the window sill. 'That's Benjy.'

Rafferty found himself face to face with the most vicious set of teeth he'd ever seen on man or beast. Beside him, smiling radiantly, with arms tightly hugging the head with the mad-looking eyes, was Diana with all the love and pride of ownership sparkling from her dull brown eyes.

'He can be a bit of a devil,' she said with a laugh, 'but I know he loves me really. He won't let anyone else ride him.' She laughed again. 'No one else wants to. But he's an old softy at heart.'

Rafferty doubted this. He wouldn't willingly have gone within six yards of the beast. How Diana Rexton could cheerfully climb on his back and trust herself to the untender mercies of the creature behind those wildly rolling eyes, was beyond him.

It was obvious that she was waiting for some words of admiration and Rafferty duly obliged. 'Magnificent beast.'

It was a mistake. 'Isn't he? Are you a horsy person, Inspector?' she asked. Before he could answer in the negative, she said, 'Come and say hello to him. He normally doesn't like strangers, but we might be lucky as he was in quite a good mood when I left him.'

With a heavy tread, he followed her out of the great hall and along a dimly lit passageway to a back door. Llewellyn was behind him. The passageway led to a quadrangle, made up of three parts house and one part stable block. Only three horses peered over the half-doors. One of them was Benjy. Rafferty had no trouble recognizing him. The horse neighed when he saw Diana, exposing those nasty teeth, much to Rafferty's discomfiture.

'Other people tell me he's an ugly-looking brute, but they're wrong. Perhaps it takes love to see his beauty? Because to me he's beautiful. I've had him since I was ten years old. He was a foal when I first got him. Even then he had a nasty temper.'

Why on earth had her father bought such an animal for his daughter? Rafferty wondered. It seemed an unwise purchase.

'I'd never trade him in for some pretty-faced gelding. He's a stallion with a stallion's pride, aren't you Benjy?' she said as they reached the stable door which, thankfully, contained the beast.

Benjy nodded his head in agreement and exposed those teeth again.

'For all that our friends say he's bad-tempered, he's sired half the foals in the county. The owners who want to put him to their mares forget what they call his devilish looks and look instead at his pedigree – King Charles out of Flanders Mare.'

She gazed at Rafferty as if she expected this lineage to mean something to him. He managed to murmur something that sounded suitably impressed and quickly passed on to the reason for their visit, worried in case she might take his fake admiration for the real thing and suggest opening the stable door so they could get better acquainted with this equine wonder.

'Mr Oldfield said you were together from four o'clock on the day of Mrs Staveley's murder and through the rest of the evening. Can you confirm that?'

'Yes, of course. Gary didn't go out at all. We spent the evening together and watched a sloppy romance on the television. Gary professes not to like such films, but he watched it till the end with me, then we went to bed.'

'I see. Have you known Mr Oldfield long?'

'Not long in time terms, I suppose. About three months. But I feel I've known him for far longer. We're soulmates and hope to marry.'

Her love for the ghastly Oldfield shone in her eyes. It was clear she was besotted. It was Benjy all over again.

'Thank you, Miss Rexton. That's all we needed. We'll leave you to Benjy now.'

She smiled and thanked him, clearly unable to hide her eagerness to get back in the stable with the horse. But good manners prevailed and she led them across the quadrangle and back down the stone passage to the nail-studded front door. She had it shut while Rafferty was still trying to find a way to express his desire to see more of the house without compromising his official role.

Disappointed, he returned to the car, knowing it was unlikely, after such unequivocal evidence, given by a woman with honesty shining from her, that he would see the inside of the manor house again.

Llewellyn dragged him back to the case.

'Did you believe the alibi she gave Mr Oldfield?' he asked, once they were back in the car.

'Oh yes,' said Rafferty. 'She struck me as transparently honest. I don't for a moment believe she was lying out of love for him, though, equally, I don't doubt she'd be willing enough to do so should it be necessary.'

Beside him, Llewellyn nodded. 'That was the impression I got, too. It sounds as if Mr Oldfield's out of the equation.'

'Yes.' Rafferty was a bit miffed at this, even though it meant he had one less suspect to investigate. There was undoubtedly something shifty and untrustworthy about Oldfield. Beneath his oh-so-smart suits and ties, he believed Oldfield to be a chancer. Witness how he'd hooked up with that poor unfortunate little rich girl. Rafferty could imagine that Oldfield would prefer flashy bleached blondes who believed in wearing clothes that showed off their bodies. And although Adrienne Staveley didn't fit into this category, from the photo Staveley had supplied and the comments of her lovers, she had been a vivacious woman, out for a good time

and probably complimentary about Oldfield's prowess as a
lover.

'It's clear Diana Rexton's head over heels in love with
Oldfield. But she seems too much of an honest soul to be
lying.'

'You don't know that,' Llewellyn pointed out. 'You really
don't know anything about her.'

'Agreed. But some things you don't need proved or laid
out like so many facts. Some things are self-evident. And her
honesty is one of them.'

Llewellyn abandoned his latest attempt at persuading
Rafferty from his impulsive convictions. Besides, it was
plain that Llewellyn shared this conviction. Hadn't he
already said so?

It was getting late. 'Home, James,' Rafferty said, 'and don't
spare the horses.' He didn't really expect Llewellyn not to
spare the horses. He always did. Not for him the thrashed
engine and squealing tyres so beloved of film and TV cops.
Llewellyn was a lover of cars and treated them with respect.
Besides, he was a cautious soul both behind the wheel and
elsewhere, so usually kept a good five miles below the speed
limit.

Back at the station, Rafferty immediately went to update
Superintendent Bradley on this latest development, keen to
get it out of the way. He had expected to find the super had
long since gone home. And was going through the motions
just in case Bradley had decided to stick around instead of
keeping office hours.

Much to his surprise, Bradley was still behind his desk:
he'd evidently been waiting for him. Rafferty quickly related
that one of their main suspects had an excellent alibi and to
ward off any criticism of how speedily or otherwise the case
was progressing, he added that it was good they'd made a
start on whittling down the suspects.

At least Bradley agreed with this. But apart from suggesting
he concentrate on whittling down a few more, he had little
to say and quickly let him go.

When he came back to the office Llewellyn was industri-
ously typing up his report of their interview with Diana Rexton.

Rafferty threw himself into his chair, still put out that he
had no excuse to slap the cuffs on Oldfield. 'I suppose it's

now down to John Staveley, his son and his mother, with the sister, Helen Ayling, coming up at the post.'

He sighed. Perhaps, after all, he shouldn't have listened to his ma when she'd pushed the police force as a career and would have done better to go into the building trade, like so many of his family.

He glanced at the round-faced clock on the wall. It was ten past nine and he said, 'It's late, Dafyd. You get off home.'

'What about you?'

'I'm going to stay here for a bit and wrestle with my wedding speech.'

'Still not finished it?' Llewellyn was his best man and had had his speech written weeks ago, much to Rafferty's annoyance.

'I've started it half a dozen times, but finished it – no.'

Once Llewellyn had left, Rafferty pulled out his notepad and picked up a pen.

'Ladies and gentlemen,' he wrote. 'Unaccustomed as I am—' No, he thought, that's no good. He scored through his first effort, chewed on his pen and, after some considerable time, began again. 'Ladies and gentlemen. What a lucky man I was to wake up this morning knowing I was going to marry Abra.' Better, he thought. But what to write next? He chewed the end of his pen again and sighed. Then he brightened and began once more. 'She's a beautiful girl, my Abra, and I want to thank her for agreeing to become my wife. I'm still surprised she decided to take me on, but she's done it now and there's no going back. Hard luck, Abra, my gorgeous wife.'

After what Sam Dally had said, he hoped he wasn't tempting fate by referring to Abra as his wife. They'd already had two major fallings out and she'd left him once – it had taken weeks for her to agree to go back to him.

Rafferty stared into space. I should say something about the bridesmaids next, he thought. But what? He threw down his pen and leaned back heavily in his chair. God, he thought, between all the churchgoing and speechifying I'll be glad when this wedding's over. Why does getting married have to be such an ordeal?

But thirty minutes later, having roughed out the rest of his speech, he rang Abra to let her know he was on his way home.

FOUR

When he finally got home it was after ten. He found that Abra had prepared one of her mixed salads with jacket potato, hardboiled egg, cheese, garlic mushrooms, sardines and the rest. It was one of his favourite meals, combining as it did so many varied flavours and although he was really too tired to eat, once he'd started he found himself eating it with his usual relish.

'I was ready for that,' he said as he cleared his plate. 'I didn't have time for any lunch today.' Not wanting Abra to think him as much of a wuss as Sam Dally clearly did, he cited lack of time as an excuse rather than a squeamish stomach. Once he'd got back to the station, he'd found he'd got past lunch.

'You should make time, Joe. It isn't good for you to go so many hours between meals.'

'I would normally, it's just that there's always so much to do at the beginning of a case. And then, this evening, I spent time on my wedding speech.'

'I hope you said some nice things about me.'

'You bet. Trouble is, it left me precious little to say about the bridesmaids.'

'Never mind about the bridesmaids,' Abra joked. 'Concentrate on your wife-to-be and you won't go far wrong.'

They stacked the dishwasher, then settled down on the settee with a glass of Jameson's each.

'So, how are you getting on with your latest murder?' Abra asked as she curled up on the settee beside him and sipped her whiskey. 'You'd better get it solved before the wedding. I don't want to find myself arriving at the church to discover there's no groom waiting for me. I'll do murder if that happens.'

Rafferty had rung her that afternoon to tell her he'd be late home. He'd given her brief details of the murder then. 'It's early days,' he told her. 'Though it's clear Adrienne Staveley's killer was known to her as there were no signs of a break in and the spy-hole in the front door allowed her to check who was knocking.'

'Strangulation. What a horrible way to die. Imagine staring into the face of your killer while they choke the life out of you.'

'Yes, it's pretty gruesome.' Rafferty took a sip of his own whiskey. 'It was fortunate that her teenage stepson didn't find her. It would have been a horrible experience for an impressionable lad.'

'As long as he didn't kill her. Perhaps it was a case of the Wicked Stepmother syndrome.'

'There's always that. But let's talk about something else. I have enough to do with violent death all day, I'd rather not have it all night as well.'

'OK. Oh, I forgot to tell you, the caterers rang. They wanted final confirmation of numbers. Nobody's cancelled, so I gave them the confirmation. The wedding seems to have crept up on us. Imagine, only three weeks to go till the big day when I'll be Mrs Rafferty. Mrs Joseph Aloysius Rafferty.'

'I wish you'd forget the Aloysius bit. I do my best to.'

'How can I? It's too delicious for words and gives me something permanent that I can tease you about.'

'I see. I'm not going to hear the end of it?'

Abra grinned. 'Not likely. I may even take to calling you Ally for short. Just don't get on my wrong side.'

The next morning Rafferty was up bright and early. He brought Abra a cup of tea and a couple of rounds of toast and made himself some cereal and toast before he set off for work.

Today, he wanted to check out Kyle Staveley's claim that he had been studying at the library during the time his stepmother was killed. He also wanted to talk to the Staveleys' neighbours. Mrs Jones had already been helpful in providing the information about Gary Oldfield's regular visits to the victim. Maybe, if he asked the right questions, there were other things she would be able to tell them.

Llewellyn came into the office then, bearing two steaming cups of tea.

'You're a welcome sight,' Rafferty told him. 'We'll get outside of this then head off to the library to check out Kyle Staveley's alibi.'

They soon finished the tea and set off. It was a grey day
with dark clouds threatening rain and a chill wind that had
Rafferty doing up his jacket. He mourned the warm sunshine
of the day before, but stoically resigned himself to the usual
British summer of four seasons in every day.

The library staff knew Kyle well as he was there most days
according to the assistant they spoke to. She was a middle-
aged woman with a kindly demeanour who clearly took an
interest in her customers. She had, she told them, been on
duty on the day of Adrienne Staveley's murder and was positive that Kyle had left the library before four thirty.

'He always sits there.' She pointed to a table near the window.
'And I noticed he wasn't there while I was shelving books.'

So Kyle's alibi had fallen at the first hurdle. Why had he
lied? And where had he gone when he'd left the library? Had
he returned home and killed his hated stepmother? If he had,
did his father know? Or had the boy kept it to himself? Either
way, they would need to speak to Kyle again and find out
why he had lied.

But before they did that, Rafferty wanted to speak to the
Staveleys' neighbour, Sarah Jones.

The threatened rain duly arrived as they walked to the car,
so they took brisk strides and reached it without getting too
wet. They drove out to Lavender Avenue. Sarah Jones was at
home and invited them in. Her kitchen was a welcoming room,
a sunny blue and yellow with pictures in similar hues on the
walls. She invited them to sit down and made tea.

Mrs Jones was a vivacious redhead. Luckily, she clearly
liked people and took an interest in them. She was a similar
age to the dead woman and told them that she had been quite
friendly with her.

'Did you like Adrienne Staveley?' Rafferty asked. Apart
from Gary Oldfield, he'd yet to speak to anyone who had.

'I like most people,' she replied. She poured boiling water
into the teapot and stirred the teabags before she brought it
to the table and took mugs out of the nearest cupboard. 'And
yes, I liked Adrienne. She could be difficult and she didn't
like it that her husband was out of work. Poor man, he felt
obliged to walk the streets to get out from under her feet. I
often saw him in town, pounding the pavement. It was a
marriage made for the good times, not the bad.'

'You told my officers that a man called Gary Oldfield was a regular visitor to the house. Did you ever meet him?'

'Yes, he was there a couple of times when I popped in to see Adrienne and she introduced us.' She poured the tea and added milk before pushing the sugar bowl towards them. Rafferty added three spoons.

'And what impression did you get of their relationship?'

She laughed. 'Definitely more than friends. You could tell from the way they looked at each other. Definitely more than friendship.'

'What did you think of Oldfield?'

'As I said, I only met him a couple of times and for no more than a few minutes each time. But I must say I thought him in love with himself rather than Adrienne. I thought he was just using her and I told her so.'

'What did she say?'

'That they were probably using each other, though I definitely got the impression that Adrienne cared more for him than he did for her.'

'Thank you.' Rafferty finished his tea, got up and fished a card out of his pocket. 'If you think of anything else, perhaps you'll ring me.'

'Of course.'

Sarah Jones showed them out. They got in the car and headed for the home of Mrs Staveley Senior to question Kyle as to why he'd lied to them.

Unfortunately, when they got there it was to learn that Kyle had returned to school that morning. Rafferty didn't want to haul the boy out of his class to question him. If he was being bullied, as Rafferty thought likely, such an action would only tend to make him more vulnerable to being picked on. The interview would wait till later.

John Staveley seemed distracted. He was upset that they wanted to speak to his son again and wanted to know why.

Rafferty was straight with him. 'Kyle lied to us, Mr Staveley. He wasn't at the library any later than four thirty. Do you know where he went?'

Staveley shook his head. 'I've no idea. But I'm sure he wasn't killing his stepmother if that's what you think. My son is a studious boy not a violent one.'

'I expect you're right, sir.'

Fortunately, Mrs Staveley Senior was out so they were spared her interruptions during the short time they spent at the house.

Rafferty told John Staveley he could return to his home whenever he wished as the scene of crime team had finished their work and he handed over the house keys. 'We'll leave you to get on with your day.' Wanting to know where the Staveleys would be, he asked, 'Will you be moving back home later?'

'I expect so.'

'Tell Kyle we'll be along this afternoon to talk to him. Tell him also that we don't want to hear any more lies. We'll see ourselves out.'

Rafferty drove and they made for the station, but he stopped off in the High Street, outside his cousin Nigel's estate agency. 'I've just got to pop in and see my cousin about our honeymoon villa,' he told Llewellyn. 'I won't be long.'

Llewellyn protested, as Rafferty had expected he would, as he had parked on a double yellow line. But Rafferty told him not to be such an old woman and slammed the car door on his protests.

Nigel was in his office, looking his usual immaculate self with his hair groomed to within an inch of its life. The outer room was deserted. No clients and no staff were in evidence.

'It's quiet here,' Rafferty commented. 'Is the downturn hitting you so badly?'

Nigel shrugged his sharp-suited shoulders. Today, he was in midnight blue. 'I'm getting by. I've had to let a couple of the staff go. The rest are at lunch.'

'I came in to pay the remainder of the money due on the honeymoon villa.'

Rafferty and Abra were renting a villa from Nigel's management company for their honeymoon. Nigel had branched out into managing foreign villas the previous year and had, surprisingly, given Rafferty a good deal. Rafferty had had a few qualms about booking the honeymoon with Nigel, but the deal was too good to pass up.

Rafferty pulled out his wallet and extracted his debit card. Nigel ran it through the machine after checking what was still owed on the booking.

'Thanks for that, coz,' said Nigel.

'Don't go using it to pay the staff wages,' Rafferty warned, only half joking.

'As if. It'll go to the clients once I've taken my cut.'

'I'll want a receipt.' Rafferty knew Nigel of old and liked to get confirmation that he'd paid full whack. Like the rest of the family, Nigel Blythe – who, before he had decided that a name-change to a more up-market moniker was indicated, had been called Jerry Kelly – didn't fight shy of ducking and diving.

'Of course.' Nigel pulled a receipt pad from the top drawer of his desk and completed it with a flourish. He tore it from the pad and handed it to Rafferty. 'There you are. One receipt, signed and dated.'

'Thanks. I'll be off. I hope the business picks up soon.'

'Me too, coz. Me too.'

Rafferty bade Nigel goodbye and made for the car. Llewellyn was getting restive about being parked on a double yellow and complained as Rafferty climbed in the car.

'All right,' Rafferty said. 'Keep your hair on. I'm back now. I was no more than a few minutes. You could always have driven round the block if you'd seen a traffic warden.'

'That's not the point. I don't like parking illegally. You know I don't. I'm a police officer. I'm meant to uphold the law, not break it. So are you.'

'Yeah, yeah.' Sighing heavily, Rafferty turned the key and they were soon on their way to the station.

When they got back it was to find more statements and reports awaiting them.

After arming themselves with tea and sandwiches from the canteen, they set to and began to read their way through them.

'I see the team have traced Michael Peacock, Adrienne Staveley's other male visitor,' said Rafferty, tapping the report in front of him. 'We must make time to see and question him.'

They finally reached the end of the paperwork. Rafferty stood up and grabbed his jacket. 'Let's go and talk to this Michael Peacock,' he said to Llewellyn.

Peacock lived in a block of flats about two hundred yards from the police station, so they left the car behind and walked.

Peacock was at home. He invited them in and offered tea. But Rafferty was all tea-ed out and he refused.

'We understand you knew Adrienne Staveley,' he began.

'Yes,' said Peacock. 'I was shocked to learn of her murder.'

'How well did you know her?'

'Pretty well. I met her two months ago. We seemed to strike a spark when we met and just carried on from there.'

'I understand you used to visit her at her home regularly.'

'Yes. I got the impression she got bored being in the house on her own all day and welcomed company.'

As long as it wasn't her husband, stepson or mother-in-law, was Rafferty's thought. 'When was the last time you saw her?'

Peacock frowned in thought. 'It must be about two weeks ago.'

'And you haven't seen her since?'

'No. As I said, it's about two weeks since we last met.'

'OK. Thank you. Perhaps you can tell us where you were two evenings ago from four to six o'clock?'

'I was working. I'm a self-employed electrician.'

Which meant he spent a lot of his time out and about and in other people's houses. They got the name and address of the client Peacock had been working for at the relevant time. Not that that would necessarily prove anything either way as tradesmen often popped out for parts without letting the client know and could be gone some time.

'We'll leave you to it, Mr Peacock, but we may need to speak to you again.'

'Yes, of course. Anytime. Let me show you out.'

They left and made for the station to pick up the car then headed for the Staveley's home to speak again to Kyle.

He was at home. John Staveley let them in and brought them into the drawing room where Kyle was slouched on a settee.

Invited to sit down by John Staveley, they sat on the armchairs opposite Kyle.

'Kyle, I imagine your father's told you that we've learned you lied to us about being at the library after four thirty,' Rafferty began. 'So where were you?'

Kyle didn't answer immediately, but after a few seconds he said, 'I was just walking around town, checking out a few shops. I wasn't in the mood for studying. It was a sunny day and I didn't feel like staying cooped up in the library.'

'Why didn't you tell us that in the first place instead of lying?'

He shrugged. 'I don't know. I suppose I was scared.'

'Why didn't you come home?'

'Because I knew she'd be here. Dad's always out all day.'

'Did you see anyone you know when you were walking?'

'No.'

Rafferty got up. 'That's all for now. But a word of advice, Kyle. Don't lie to the police, as you'll inevitably get found out.'

Kyle didn't answer.

John Staveley saw them to the front door.

'What now?' Rafferty asked as they got in the car and headed back to the station. 'We seem to be hitting dead ends all the way.'

'We're fairly certain that Adrienne Staveley was killed by someone who knew her,' said Llewellyn. 'It's surely just a matter of sifting through her family, friends and acquaintances. We'll get there.'

'I hope you're right. I'm not optimistic. Anyway, let's get back to the station and type up these last two interviews. When we get there, remind me to get one of the team to check out Peacock's client to see if they can confirm he was there between four and six o'clock.'

The journey back to the station was quickly accomplished. Soon they were ensconced in their office with Llewellyn busy typing up his notes. The phone rang. It was the estate agent Rafferty and Abra were using to sell their respective flats – he had chosen not to use his cousin's services: Nigel was just too tricksy for such a major matter.

'I've got a viewing for you,' the estate agent told Rafferty.

'Great. When for?'

'This evening at seven thirty.'

'That's fine. Thanks.' Rafferty put the phone down. It was only the third viewing he'd had; the property market was still slow moving after the recession. It was a fag keeping the place tidy, but if it sold it would be all to the good.

The rest of the day passed slowly. Hanks who had been deputed to speak to Peacock's client reported that the client hadn't been able to confirm Peacock's alibi as the electrician had left the house for half an hour during the relevant time.

Superintendent Bradley stopped by to discover what

progress they'd made and wasn't best pleased to learn they seemed to be getting nowhere.

'It's a limited circle of suspects,' he said. 'You must have someone who sticks out.'

'No one that springs to mind,' Rafferty replied.

'What about the husband? You said he didn't have an alibi worthy of the name.'

'He's a possible, certainly. But as yet we've no proof of guilt.'

'Well get some, Rafferty, get some. And soon. I want this case wrapped up as quickly as possible. Murder cases eat into my budget. You know I like to present a clean pair of financial heels at Region.'

Rafferty did. He'd had it hammered into his head at regular intervals.

Bradley stomped off.

Rafferty sighed and went back to reading the latest statements. But there was nothing of interest in any of them. He sighed again and sat back. If only Bradley wouldn't be so unreasonable in his demands. But his desire to impress the brass at Region made him behave unfairly to those under him. A leader of men he wasn't.

The rest of the day dragged by and Rafferty was glad when it ended and he could go home. It had rained earlier and the car park was awash with puddles. He wove his way through them to the car.

Abra was back at the flat before him. They had a quick, microwaved meal before the potential flat purchaser arrived.

The viewer was right on time. He seemed to like the flat and also appeared enthusiastic about the amenities in the area.

'Looks hopeful,' said Rafferty after he'd shown their potential buyer out.

'Yes,' said Abra. 'He seemed keen enough. Let's hope it comes to something. It'll be good to get a firm offer on one of our flats before the wedding.' She paused, then asked, 'Do you want to do anything this evening?'

'No. Achieving nothing all day has made me tired. It's the frustration that does it.'

They had a lazy, relaxed evening in front of the television and went to bed before ten.

*   *   *

The next morning Rafferty was again up early. He brought
Abra her tea and drank his own sitting at the kitchen table.
He left for work earlier than usual and for once arrived before
Llewellyn.

The estate agent rang him just after nine and told him that
their viewer of the previous night had been in touch and had
made an offer. It was a good one, not far off the asking price
and Rafferty was happy to accept it.

Llewellyn arrived. He went and got their morning tea and
then they got to work reading the latest reports. But again
there was nothing of interest. The case seemed to be stalemated.

The forensic reports had come in. Adrienne Staveley's
fingernails had been checked to see if her attacker's skin
was caught under them. But forensic had discovered nothing.
There had been a number of fingerprints found in the kitchen,
including those of Gary Oldfield and Michael Peacock, as
well as several unknown ones. One lot was probably those
of the Staveleys' neighbour. They'd asked her to come into
the station to have her prints taken. Rafferty had also put
out a request asking for anyone who had come to the house
and who might have had access to the kitchen to come
forward.

He'd yet to look through Adrienne Staveley's personal
effects: he must do that as a priority. With this thought in
mind, he summoned two of the team, Gerry Hanks and Timothy
Smales, to his office and gave them instructions to search the
Staveleys' house with particular emphasis on Adrienne's
bedroom. That done, he sat back and contemplated what else
he had yet to do.

He had told Hanks to get John Staveley's permission to
take one of the photographs of Adrienne for copying. He
needed to circulate it to the news media in case anyone could
pinpoint her as meeting with any other men locally. They
needed to find out the names of all of her friends and acquaintances in order to be able to eliminate them – or not as the
case might be. Somebody in her life that they had yet to find
out about could have killed her and their concentration on the
current crop of suspects may be all for nothing.

'Helen Ayling told us that Adrienne was a woman who
liked to flirt,' he said to Llewellyn. 'Maybe she went too far

in her flirting while withholding her favours to one of the men in her life.'

'It's a possibility,' Llewellyn conceded. 'But we shouldn't rule anything out yet.'

'I'm not. I'm keeping an open mind.'

Llewellyn's lips tilted fractionally upwards at this and Rafferty scowled.

'I am,' he insisted. 'But it's always advisable to consider the victim's character – it often points the way to the reason for their murder.'

'I don't disagree. Mrs Staveley's character is an important aspect. Just not the only one.'

'I know that. Me, I think the husband's favourite rather than one of her men friends. He certainly had sufficient motive.'

'Yes. It seems to have been a less than happy marriage, at least lately. Though you'd think he'd have arranged an alibi.'

'Perhaps he hasn't got any friends loyal enough to be prepared to lie for him, particularly in a murder case.'

'Perhaps not. But I would have thought his mother or sister might have alibied him, particularly his mother, as she struck me as the sort of woman who would be behind her son right or wrong.'

'Yes. She struck me that way too. I wonder why John Staveley *didn't* arrange for her to lie for him.'

'It could be a pointer to his innocence.'

'Or a pointer to the desire to make us think that,' said Rafferty. 'He strikes me as a deep one, fully capable of such double-thinking in order to muddy the waters.'

'Time will tell.'

'Time. And to listen to Superintendent Bradley, time isn't on our side.'

'It never is in a murder inquiry. But rushing ahead of the evidence to please the superintendent or anyone else is always a mistake. We need to make haste slowly.'

'Make haste slowly,' Rafferty scoffed. 'How I hate those old wiseacres and their glib advice. How can you make haste slowly? It's a contradiction in terms. Anyway,' he said before Llewellyn could come back with a glib riposte of his own, 'to change the subject – how are you getting on with the arrangements for my stag do? I hope you're not organizing a trip to the theatre to see Shakespeare or something equally highbrow.'

'Of course not. I know Shakespeare's not your sort of thing and it is *your* night. No. Don't worry. I'm organizing something more to your taste.'

'I hope so.' Rafferty had misgivings about letting Llewellyn arrange his stag night. But the Welshman *was* his best man and it was tradition that it fell to the best man to get the stag do sorted. He still had a niggle of doubt that Llewellyn would arrange something appropriate, but he had no choice but to take it on trust.

He turned the conversation back to the murder. 'Killing by strangulation is often an act of rage, especially, as we suspect, if it's by someone who knew the victim. Maybe if we can find out who had reason to be angry with her, we might find her murderer.'

'Which brings us back to her husband.'

'It does, doesn't it? Certainly, as I said, he's my favourite at the moment.'

'What about the victim's stepson?'

'Certainly, there was no love lost there. He's a wiry lad and tall for his age. I should think he's physically capable of strangling someone. And when you add in all that teenage angst . . .'

Late that afternoon, Hanks and Smales returned from searching the Staveleys' house. Smales, as he produced an A5 size diary, was particularly triumphant. The bum fluff whiskers on his youthful face gleamed as a shaft of sunlight shot through the window. 'We found this, sir. It's the victim's diary.'

'Well done. Have you looked at it? Does it contain anything interesting?'

Smales's face fell. 'I don't know, sir. It's all written in what looks like shorthand.'

Rafferty tutted in frustration. 'Still,' he said, 'it points to her having secrets worth confiding to her diary.' He turned to Llewellyn. 'I don't suppose you number shorthand amongst your many talents?'

'I'm afraid not. Somehow I missed out on that one.'

'Oh, well. We'll have to find someone to transcribe it for us. Maybe the super's secretary does shorthand.'

'There was something else interesting, sir,' said Hanks. 'Mr and Mrs Staveley didn't share a bedroom.'

'Did they not?' Rafferty glanced at Llewellyn. 'Another pointer to the estrangement between them. I wonder how long they've been sleeping apart. OK, lads, thanks. You've done well. Get back out and see if you can discover Adrienne Staveley's haunts locally. You picked up a photograph from her home?'

Hanks nodded.

'See if you can find anyone who saw her wining, dining or lunching with a man. Or even just having a coffee with one. And don't lose that photo – I want it to make copies for general circulation. Off you go.'

Hanks and Smales left and Rafferty turned to Llewellyn. 'Wonder what the diary will tell us.'

'It's certainly intriguing that she wrote it in shorthand.'

'That's what I thought. There might be a feast of information in there. Maybe it'll even appease Bradley's desire for fast results.'

FIVE

B ut the diary took some time to transcribe and Rafferty – and Superintendent Bradley – had to bear their souls in patience. Meanwhile, he had Adrienne Staveley's photo circulated to the media in the hope that someone had seen her with one or more of the men in her life and could provide a description of any men friends of whom they were as yet unaware.

Hanks and Tim Smales, between them, had already discovered a few interesting sightings of Adrienne Staveley in town with different men. One of them, from the description, sounded like Gary Oldfield, but the other one was unidentified. It wasn't Michael Peacock because he had a shock of fair hair and the other man had been described as having brown hair and an earring. Rafferty had told the pair to keep trying; it was possible they would yet find out the other man's identity.

Adrienne Staveley had been quite a girl, he thought and wondered if they'd find any other men who'd had a relationship with her.

Meanwhile, Rafferty and Abra's wedding date was drawing closer. Abra was becoming increasingly anxious that they'd have to postpone that or the honeymoon and Rafferty, bogged down in a case that seemed to be going nowhere, found it more and more difficult to reassure her.

'Why don't you ask to have more men assigned to the case?' she asked Rafferty when he brought her morning tea. 'Surely more bodies would help bring it to a quicker conclusion?'

'Possibly. But I can't see Superintendent Bradley letting me have more officers – there are other cases on our books that also require a solution and the police budget's been cut, so there's less money to throw at cases. No, I'll have to carry on with the bodies I've got and hope something breaks.'

'Hope,' Abra scoffed. 'I hoped that this wedding would go off without a hitch. Fat chance now, with this murder hanging over us.'

'Don't say that, sweetheart. We've time yet for the case to

be solved. *Nil desperandum*, as Dafyd would say.' Llewellyn had a habit of coming out with Latin phrases, much to Rafferty's irritation. He was amused to find himself doing likewise.

'It's all right for him – he didn't have to postpone *his* wedding.'

'And neither do we, yet. Anyway, there's no reason why the wedding itself should need to be postponed. I can always take a few hours off to tie the knot.'

'And what about the honeymoon?' she asked. 'I hope you took out insurance in case we have to cancel.'

He hadn't. But he didn't tell Abra that. 'Leave it with me, sweetheart. I'll speak to Nigel.' He had booked the honeymoon through his estate agent cousin who had a sideline as the agent for various continental villas. The idea of insurance hadn't been mentioned by either of them. 'Don't keep looking on the black side,' Rafferty told her. 'You'll attract bad luck.'

Abra pulled a face, but said nothing more and Rafferty made his escape before she had the chance to ask any further unwelcome questions about the non-existent insurance. If it came to it, he'd just have to stump up the money for another honeymoon later on as he couldn't see Nigel giving him a refund even though they were cousins. Family didn't count for much with Nigel, unfortunately.

Rafferty finished his tea and toast and headed for the station with Abra's words reverberating around his head. He didn't know how to appease her. The only way would be for him to solve his current case and that didn't look likely at the moment.

He found that little new had come in when he got to work, and what little there was Llewellyn was sorting through, leaving Rafferty to watch and twiddle his thumbs.

'Anything of interest?' he finally asked after Llewellyn had failed to volunteer any information.

Llewellyn looked up and shook his head. 'Bottom of the barrel stuff.'

'You might as well get the teas in, then.' Rafferty put his hand in his pocket, found a pound coin and flicked it to Llewellyn.

Once Llewellyn had gone off to the canteen, Rafferty glanced through the latest reports on the Welshman's desk. But as Dafyd had said, there was nothing of any interest there.

Llewellyn came back with the tea and they drank it in silence, Rafferty pondering what to do next. He asked Llewellyn, 'Have we had anything in yet from the roadside patrol I set up?' He had organized a roadside survey on the main road nearest to the turn off to the Staveleys' side road in the hope that someone had seen a car going up there before the murder or returning afterwards. But Llewellyn told him nothing had yet come in.

Rafferty was fed up with the stalemate situation; he wanted to be up and doing.

'Find out how the super's secretary is getting on with transcribing Adrienne Staveley's diary, will you, Dafyd? She must have done some by now, no matter how demanding the old man is.'

Ten minutes later, Rafferty had the transcript that had so far been typed. There were some gaps in it and Llewellyn explained them.

'It seems shorthand writers develop their own short forms for some words and the superintendent's secretary didn't want to guess and perhaps make a mistake. Also, she said Mrs Staveley's shorthand must have been a bit rusty as her outlines weren't always terribly accurate. She says she did the best she could.'

Rafferty had told Anne, the super's secretary, to start on the part of the diary that was written in the month before Adrienne's murder. Adrienne clearly hadn't been a prolific diary writer: for some days there were no entries at all and for others just a few lines. But on some dates she had gone in for more detailed entries.

'Listen to this,' said Rafferty. '"*Met Mike at the Black Swan and had a great meal. Came back home and had an exhausting sex session. He's almost as good a lover as Gary. Can't wait till next week when we meet again.*"' He flipped over the page and said, 'Here's another one. "*Gary came over at lunchtime and we went to bed. Two* blank *hours. He really is very inventive. Great* blank *and even greater cock*". I bet the super's secretary got hot under the collar when she read that.' The super's secretary, Anne Amos, was a fifty-something spinster.

'At least we have it confirmed that Gary Oldfield and Michael Peacock were her lovers,' Llewellyn commented.

'Yes. Although Peacock didn't lie to us about being

Adrienne's lover, Oldfield did. Just good friends, he said, or words to that effect. We'll have to question the pair again now that we're armed with this new information. I know Diana Rexton alibied him, but, given that he lied to us about the nature of his relationship with Adrienne Staveley, I think he's worth questioning again.'

Rafferty read through the rest of the transcript. It seemed that Adrienne's relationship with Oldfield was more serious than the one with Peacock. She appeared to have been pushing him to set up home with her, but Oldfield was proving reluctant. 'I wonder if John Staveley suspected any of this,' he commented after he read out the relevant part of the diary to Llewellyn.

'What is it they say? That it's always the husband who's the last to know.'

'Still, going on under his nose in his own house and I presume in what was once the marital bed – it makes you think. I can't wait to read the rest of the transcripts. We might learn the identity of the mysterious third man she was seen with.'

'I doubt it.' Llewellyn poured cold water on his hopes. 'So far, she's only used first names.'

'Well, we might get lucky. Let's go and see Oldfield and Peacock and find out if we can't get them to admit they were her lovers. Faced with this transcript I don't see how they can deny it.'

One look out of the window told Rafferty that the day had turned even more wet and blustery so he threw on his jacket before they went to see Gary Oldfield. They found him at the used car lot where he worked. He was sharply dressed as he had been the last time they had seen him and today sported a pair of flashy cufflinks – gold with silver detail and a raised red pattern of what looked like a Bentley.

When Rafferty told him that they knew from Adrienne Staveley's diary that he had been her lover, his previous line of ready chat dried up and he became far more reticent. Luckily for him, his girlfriend had confirmed that Oldfield had been with her during the two-hour period covering the time when Sam Dally had said Adrienne Staveley had been murdered.

Still he had failed to tell them something that might turn

out to be relevant to the inquiry and Rafferty waved the relevant page of the transcript under his nose. 'It's all in here,' he said. 'Apparently, Mrs Staveley admired your sexual technique.'

This brought a grin to Oldfield's face. 'Nice to be appreciated.'

'I also understand she was pushing you to move your relationship up a notch: she wanted you to set up home together.'

'That was never going to happen, she knew that. I'd made it clear enough. Adrienne was good for a fling, but that was as far as it went. She knows I'm with Diana and that, in spite of her parents' opposition, we hope to marry.'

His girlfriend, Diana Rexton, had come as a surprise to Rafferty: very plain and homely, with what he called a shapeless figure, her love for Oldfield had shone out of her plain face. Rafferty would have suspected her of lying about Oldfield's whereabouts at the time of the murder, but she was so transparently honest that he had believed her when she had agreed that he had been with her. He wished he hadn't. Still she might be mistaken. She could have fallen asleep, enabling him to slip out for half an hour. He hadn't asked her if that was a possibility. Maybe he should. It was quite likely that she wouldn't attempt to lie to him and even if she did, her natural honesty wouldn't allow her to do so convincingly. But that was for another time. Right now it was Oldfield he was questioning.

'So you admit that you and she were having an affair?'

'Doesn't look like I've got much choice. Yes, we were sleeping together, though there wasn't a lot of sleeping going on.' Oldfield grinned again. 'She was a bit of a goer, Adrienne. I doubt I was her only lover.'

Rafferty didn't mention Michael Peacock or the third as yet unidentified male. They were none of Oldfield's business. Maybe Adrienne had pressed Oldfield harder than he admitted for them to set up home together and it had all gone sour. He had the feeling that Oldfield had a nasty streak and wouldn't hesitate to resort to physical violence if he thought it necessary.

'How often did you and Mrs Staveley get together for sex?'

'Once or twice a week, depending on my hours.'

'And how long had your affair been going on?'

'Around five months.'

So only one month after her husband had been made redundant Adrienne had turned to another man for solace. It didn't say much for her loyalty. But then the transcripts of her diary had already made that more than clear.

'Well, thank you for being so frank, Mr Oldfield. We may need to speak to you again.'

Oldfield shrugged his sharply suited shoulders. 'You know where to find me.'

'Yes, we do, don't we? Come along, Llewellyn, let's not take up any more of Mr Oldfield's valuable time.'

Their car was parked at the kerb right outside the used car lot and they were soon on their way to see Michael Peacock. But this time they were unlucky. He wasn't home. They would have to come back that evening.

'Let's get along to the roadside survey team and see how they're getting on,' said Rafferty. 'They might have something by now and I don't want to wait for them to make their report.'

The roadside team had a queue of cars lined up awaiting their attention.

Rafferty parked up and strolled over to the head of the queue where the officers were questioning a lady driver. 'How's it going lads?' he asked.

'Slowly sir,' said the officer clutching the clipboard. He was new to the team and Rafferty was unable to recall his name. 'So far no one's admitted to seeing a car either going or coming from that side road.'

Rafferty pulled a face. 'What – nobody at all?'

The officer shook his head.

Rafferty had hoped for more as they had precious little to go on. They had a number of contenders for the role of murderer, but, so far, no strong evidence against any of them.

Rafferty was grumpy as they returned to the car and headed for the station. 'I suppose I can expect Bradley to bawl me out again when we get back. God, but he's an unreasonable old bugger.'

'He was ever one for impressing Region with quick results,' said Llewellyn and he pulled up – unnecessarily in Rafferty's opinion – at the amber light showing at the traffic lights, changed into neutral and put the brake on. They could easily have made it through if Llewellyn had only put his foot down.

It was unlike Llewellyn to criticize others, particularly a senior officer, and Rafferty turned to him in surprise. 'What brought that on?'

'Perhaps I got out of bed on the wrong side. But I agree with you that Superintendent Bradley can be unreasonable. By his unhelpful attitude he just puts more, unnecessary, pressure on the team.'

'Hallelujah! Finally, I've got you to let your hair down and say what you really think of our esteemed leader. Can I have it in writing? I'll get it framed.'

'It's never a good idea to put such opinions in writing. One never knows when they'll come back to haunt one.'

Rafferty laughed. 'One's right,' he mimicked. 'One doesn't. Still,' he added, 'it's good to know you agree with me. It makes me feel better.'

Superintendent Bradley gave him the expected bawling out, but this time Rafferty took it with a pinch of salt, comforted by the fact that Llewellyn also thought Bradley an unsupportive twat even though he had chosen a more polite way to say it. Bradley must have kissed some arses at Region to make it to the rank of superintendent. Rafferty hoped he caught something from the next one he kissed.

Rafferty was due to take his ma shopping that evening. He normally took her every week. He considered putting it off as he'd already had a long day, but decided against it. It wouldn't be fair as his ma looked forward to his visits and to him taking her to the supermarket.

As always, she was ready when he rang her doorbell, her permed hair just so and the waft of hairspray coming off her. 'Hello, son,' she said. 'Looking forward to your big day?'

'Yes, but I've been getting the collywobbles about making my speech.'

'Go on, you'll be fine. Just imagine you're talking to young Tim Smales. There's nothing to be frightened of there, is there?'

'Little Timmy Smales? No. No. You're right. I'll keep Smales in mind. Shall we go?'

'Yes. I'm ready.'

They went out to the car and Rafferty helped her in and tucked her skirt around her.

The supermarket wasn't far and the shopping soon done as ma always wrote a list and was very efficient and not easily distracted by eye-catching offers.

Rafferty drove her home again and went in for a cup of tea and a sandwich.

Ma bustled about in the kitchen. She quickly reappeared bearing his tea and beef sandwiches.

Rafferty took a huge bite 'Mmm, these are beautiful, Ma.'

'They should be, with the price of beef. I only buy it occasionally when it's on special offer at the butchers.'

'How are you managing? I can let you have a bit more money if you need it.' Rafferty put money into his ma's bank account regularly each month as did his two brothers.

'No, son, I'm all right. I can't expect you to fork out more with your wedding so close. You're good enough to me as it is. Besides, I manage very well on the whole. I'm good at managing, after being widowed with six kids to feed and clothe, I've had to be.'

She sat down and nursed her own tea. 'So how's Abra? Not getting cold feet?'

There was that question again. Did everyone else know something he didn't? he wondered. 'No, she's fine. Looking forward to the wedding as I am, though she's worried we'll have to postpone the honeymoon.'

'Oh, honeymoons. They're overrated in my experience. On our wedding night your father went to the pub and forgot to come back to the room. I spent the entire night on my own and was woken at six o'clock by the landlady complaining that my husband was fast asleep on her doorstep.'

Rafferty laughed. He'd heard this story before, but it still amused him. He could just picture his father curled up, quite comfortably, on his landlady's doorstep. He imagined he wasn't quite so comfortable when roused and treated to his ma's acerbic tongue, which he thought likely to be as capable of giving a deserved lashing then as it was today. He could almost feel sorry for his old man. Still, he'd been wrong to stay out till the early hours on his wedding night. His poor ma must have felt horribly embarrassed. Not much of a start to married life. At least his wouldn't start in such a way.

'So, how have you been, Ma? You're keeping well? How's my great-nephew?' His niece, Gemma, had had a son, whom she had named Joseph as a compliment to him, though the family all called him Joey. She was a young, unmarried mother and she and the child lived with her mother, Maggie, Rafferty's sister.

'I'm fine,' his ma told him. 'And little Joey's blooming and growing fast. You ought to make time to go and see them.'

'I will, Ma, as soon as this case is over.' The things he was going to do when this case was over.

'How are your sandwiches?'

'Delicious,' said Rafferty again as he finished the last one. His ma always stuffed him with food when he came to see her and always wanted praise for her servings. Rafferty, replete, was happy to oblige her.

'I get the beef from the butchers on the High Street. They're independents and their meat's always reliable.' She finished her tea and sat back. 'I hope you get your latest case solved before your honeymoon.'

So did Rafferty. 'Yes, if I don't I might have to cancel.'

'Still, you'll be insured and can go later in the year.' She looked at him over her spectacles and asked, 'You are insured, I take it.'

The expression on his too open face must have given him away. 'Not exactly, no.'

'I suppose that means you're not. Really, Joseph, that was careless of you.'

'I know. It just completely left my head to do it. Don't tell Abra. She doesn't know.'

Luckily, his ma didn't believe in the doctrine that couples shouldn't have secrets from one another. She thought they probably *should* if they were to stay married. She'd certainly kept plenty of secrets from Rafferty's dad, from what she'd paid for their clothes to what Christmas had cost her. The things his dad hadn't known were legion; the refrain, 'don't tell your father', had often been on his ma's lips. And they hadn't told him. They'd learned to be good at keeping secrets, too. Except for him. His open face gave him away more often than not.

'Another cup of tea, Joe?'

'Please.'

His ma took his mug and disappeared into the kitchen. She was soon back, bearing his fresh mug of tea.

Mostly, Rafferty enjoyed visiting his ma, but occasionally, she gave him as good a tongue-lashing as she'd given his late father. He half-expected one as he casually asked her, 'Bought anything from the market recently?' But the expected sharp riposte didn't come. His ma had a habit of buying question-able items from the local street market. He hadn't been able to cure her of it. These knocked-off purchases had originated when she'd been widowed and money was tight and continued to this day. Sometimes, her purchases had put his police career in jeopardy, but, much as she loved him and wanted to do well by him, even that hadn't stopped her. It was a contin-uing worry for him.

'I bought Joey a warm coat for the winter. A real bargain. And a bike for his birthday.'

That was the trouble – his ma's purchases usually were 'bargains' and for a very good reason. Stolen goods were often a bargain simply because they'd been stolen.

'Gemma will be pleased.' He wished he were. 'Thanks for the tea and sandwiches, Ma. I'd better be off now or Abra'll think I've run away from home.'

'OK, son. See you next week. And stop worrying about your wedding speech. It's sure I am that you'll be fine.'

He kissed her and made for the door. The drive home was quick and uneventful. Luckily, Abra hadn't made a start on dinner as his ma's thick sandwiches had filled him up.

'Your mother all right?' she asked after he came into the kitchen and put the kettle on.

'Yes. She's in fine fettle. Looking forward to the wedding. I reckon I was lucky to escape a demonstration of her wedding finery. Thank God I've got three sisters for such duties.'

Abra laughed. 'Come on, Ally, make the tea. You can make me a sandwich while you're at it.'

'Yes, Ma'am. Whatever you say.' Rafferty made the tea and opened the door of the fridge. 'Cheese and tomato OK?'

Abra nodded.

The sandwiches didn't take long to make and soon they repaired to the living room.

'So how was your day?' Abra asked as she peered at him over her mug.

Even though she hadn't asked, he knew what she meant.
It was – was he any nearer to solving the murder? He wasn't,
but was reluctant to admit it again. 'It was OK, sweetheart.
Spoke to a lot of possible witnesses; read a lot of reports and
statements. The usual stuff. How about you?'

'Oh, busy, as usual. The bosses want to freeze our pay for
a year with this recession – so much for it being over.
Everyone's up in arms as you might imagine. God knows,
they don't pay us a lot now.'

'So what are you going to do about it?'

'We're thinking of going on strike.'

'Really? Won't they bring in temporary staff? Strike breakers?'

'Yes. That's the trouble. And there aren't enough of us to
make an effective picket line. The talk about strike action is
probably so much hot air. I think the bosses are looking for
an excuse to cut staff and want to weed out troublemakers.'

'Like you?'

Abra grinned. 'Yes, like me. Not that I think I'm a trou-
blemaker, as such. It's just that I believe in sticking up for
myself and they don't like it. Remember the time I threatened them with a lawyer when they were less than complimentary about my attitude and team spirit in my yearly
appraisal?'

Rafferty did. That one had gone to the wire, but the bosses
had drawn back just before Abra made good her threat.

Abra worked as a secretary in a theatrical agency and
was often full of tales of their more troublesome clients.
Some of them were very demanding and sometimes caused
scenes at the offices. They had some well-known and high-
earning names on their books and the firm made a good
income. That was why Rafferty was surprised to learn they
wanted to impose a pay freeze. It was typical boss behaviour to Rafferty's mind. He admired his fiancée for her
previous bold stance, though he hoped she didn't find reason
to make it again: At least not this year. With the wedding
and the new house they were hoping to buy they needed
all the money they could lay their hands on and Abra being
either sacked or on strike was the last thing he wanted. It
wasn't as if she was in a union and would receive strike
pay.

Abra finished her sandwiches and asked Rafferty if he

minded if she put the TV on. 'Only there's a documentary I want to watch,' she explained.

'Feel free, sweetheart. I'm easy.'

'Yes. I'd heard that,' Abra joked. She turned the television on and they settled down for an evening's viewing. Or at least Abra did.

Rafferty was pleased to sink into sloth. He was tired and was glad of the opportunity to catch forty winks while Abra watched her programme. Maybe he'd dream the answer to the murder.

SIX

Rafferty hadn't got around to seeing Michael Peacock the previous evening, so they went the next night after the routine jobs of the day were done. Peacock was, as they'd already discovered, a totally different proposition to Gary Oldfield. He lacked Oldfield's cocky air. In fact he was rather diffident and dressed down, rather than up, like Oldfield. Rafferty was surprised he'd taken Adrienne's fancy; he'd have thought the electrician – given that she'd gone for Gary Oldfield – far too casually dressed for her tastes. When they went to question him he had obviously not long come in from work and was wearing scruffy jeans and a dirty T-shirt.

When questioned and shown the diary extract, Peacock freely admitted that he had been having an affair with Adrienne Staveley.

'I wasn't proud of it,' he said, as he brushed his thick fair hair back from his brow, with a hand that showed the marks of honest labour. 'But there was just something about Adrienne. She made me feel alive, like no girlfriend I've had before. She was exciting.'

'And what about her husband?' Rafferty asked. 'Did you ever meet him?'

'No, thank God. I wouldn't have known what to say to him. I felt bad about sleeping with his wife, but I just couldn't help myself. She was like a drug to me. I couldn't get enough of her.'

'You realize this makes you a suspect, Mr Peacock?'

'Does it? I hadn't thought about it. I didn't kill her. I would never have done that, she meant too much to me. She transformed my life, gave me a reason for living. My life was pretty humdrum before I met her. She introduced me to all sorts of things: the theatre, books, even ballet, though I'm not so keen on that.'

'And how did you meet?'

'I'm an electrician, as I told you last time you questioned me. She called me in to fix a faulty socket and it just progressed from there.'

'What? You mean she slept with you that same day? The
day she met you?'

'Yes. I was shocked, but willing. As I said, she was an
exciting lady. I couldn't believe my luck. Me a humble electrician and her so much a cut above.'

Probably her bit of rough, was Rafferty's thought. Poor
John Staveley; he had been well and truly cuckolded, first
with Gary Oldfield and then with Peacock. Rafferty wondered
when Adrienne fitted in the third, mystery man. He wouldn't
have blamed Staveley if he *had* killed his wife. He'd certainly
had enough provocation.

Rafferty didn't think the diffident, couldn't believe his luck,
Michael Peacock had killed Adrienne, but of course, he
couldn't yet be scratched from the list of suspects. For all he
knew Peacock was a very good liar.

They took their leave and returned to the station –
Llewellyn to type up his notes of the interview and Rafferty
to collect his car and drive to see his cousin, Nigel. The
estate agent's was closed so he drove to Nigel's swanky
warehouse apartment.

Luckily, Nigel was in and for a change even seemed quite
welcoming. Normally, he didn't like members of his family
turning up unannounced at his apartment.

'So what can I do for you, coz,' he asked once they were
seated in his huge lounge.

'It's about the honeymoon,' Rafferty began. 'I'm still on
this murder case and I wondered what chance I stand for a
refund if I have to cancel.'

Nigel laughed. 'No chance. No chance at all, my old son.'

'That's a bit harsh.'

'You might not have noticed, but it's a harsh world out
there.'

'And in here.'

'I've a living to make, Joseph, the same as you. It's not as
if you took out any insurance.'

'You never mentioned insurance.'

'Neither did you. Though you might check your household
insurance; that could cover you.'

'Really?' Rafferty doubted it; he believed it was only for
luggage that his home insurance would give cover. It was typical
of Nigel to try to wriggle out from under any accountability

by claiming Rafferty could get his money back from someone other than himself.

'As I said, it might. You want to check your policy documents.'

'I'll do that.' Though how he was supposed to do that with Abra there. She'd be bound to ask why he was checking them.

'So – do you want me to cancel the honeymoon?'

'No. Not yet. It might still be on. It all depends on this latest case.'

'Well, don't leave it too late. If I can offload the villa on to some other punter you might be able to get some of your money back, though I wouldn't bet on finding another customer this late in the day.'

Disgruntled, Rafferty left his cousin's apartment and headed home, hoping that Abra didn't think again to question him about the insurance position.

But thankfully, when he got home it was to discover that something other than the insurance for their honeymoon was preoccupying her. It seemed that one of her three bridesmaids had gone down with glandular fever.

'Does it matter?' Rafferty asked. 'Can't you make do with two bridesmaids? I'll only have the one best man.'

'It's not the same thing at all,' Abra told him with some asperity: it was clear she'd had a fraught day over this. 'Besides, the dresses cost a fortune. It'll be a total waste if one of them doesn't even get worn.'

'How long does glandular fever last?' he asked. 'We've still over two weeks till the big day.'

'I've spent a chunk of the day when I should have been working checking it out on the internet.'

Rafferty just managed to refrain from pointing out that this was something her employers might take exception to if they caught her. Abra sometimes courted dismissal, he suspected, just as he wasn't totally averse from courting Superintendent Bradley's umbrage.

'And what did you find out?'

'It could take several months for her to get well – though the consensus seems to be that that's a worse case scenario, but it doesn't seem likely that she'll be well enough for our wedding. Apparently, glandular fever induces extreme fatigue amongst other symptoms. Usually it takes between two to four weeks to resolve itself.'

'Well, it's not the end of the world. It would be different if it had been you or me that had caught it.'

'I knew you wouldn't understand. It'll ruin the pictures of me with the bridesmaids. I wanted the two little ones to stand in front, matched like two peas.'

Abra had chosen her younger sister and two little nieces as bridesmaids. If this was the result after losing one of the little ones, Rafferty could only hope the other one didn't catch the virus.

Abra wasn't to be consoled. He hadn't seen any dinner preparations going on in the kitchen, so he suggested he go out for a takeaway.

'Trust you to think of your stomach.'

'Well, as I see it, we can do nothing about the bridesmaid problem unless you've got another niece or cousin who's the same size as the one with the fever. But I *can* do something about dinner.'

He quickly shrugged back into his jacket, gave Abra a peck on the cheek and told her he wouldn't be long. He was glad to escape. Abra in this mood could be difficult to appease. She tended to take things to heart no matter how illogical, as evidenced by this bridesmaid saga. For the life of him, he couldn't see what difference it made if Abra had three bridesmaids or two or none at all. That would have been better, in his opinion. It would certainly have cut down on some of the costs. But that was a point of view he now rarely allowed himself to indulge just in case he blurted it out and she left him again. Perhaps she'd feel better with some food inside her.

Thankfully, by the time he returned, half an hour later, she seemed less upset. He dished up the meal and quietly handed her a glass of Jameson's. They ate the Indian in companionable silence, with just a CD compilation of Rafferty's favourite sixties' music playing in the background.

'Do you feel a bit better now?' Rafferty asked as they finished their meal.

Abra nodded. 'A bit. I've been thinking. I suppose I could ask my youngest cousin, Aimee; she's about the same size as Sophie.'

'There you are then. All's well that ends well. I doubt any necessary alterations would take long.'

'No. You're right. It was silly of me to get so upset.'

'It's understandable. It's a fraught business arranging a wedding. There's always so much that can go wrong.'

'Oh God, Joe, don't say that. I'll be worrying about what else can happen.'

'Nothing will.' Rafferty crossed his fingers under the table out of Abra's sight. 'You'll see I'm right. It'll be plain sailing from here on in.' He took a bite of a poppadom and scooped up the rest of his Chicken Tikka Masala, Abra's favourite Indian meal.

They had an early night because after getting herself worked into such a state, Abra felt exhausted.

It was a long time before Rafferty fell asleep. His mind churned with the difficulties of his latest case. Who was the murderer? The husband? One of her lovers? Her mother or sister-in-law? The stepson? He felt sure *one* of them was guilty.

The husband, John Staveley, was still his favourite, but he must make sure this didn't blind him to other possibilities. He wished he could be as objective as Llewellyn. His sergeant seemed to have no problem in keeping an open mind, which was something that caused Rafferty endless difficulties. He tended to home in on one particular suspect to the exclusion of the rest. It was about time he learned not to do that.

He turned over and thumped his pillow. Come on, sleep, he muttered to himself. I'll be like nothing on earth tomorrow if you don't come and in no fit state to find answers with or without an open mind.

Rafferty woke late and unrefreshed the next morning. With a groan, he levered himself out of bed and walked to the bathroom. A shower partially revived him as did tea and fried egg on toast. Maybe today, Anne Amos would get some more of Adrienne Staveley's diary transcribed. And Bradley was spending the day at Region doing more arse licking so he wouldn't be causing him any further angst.

Fed and watered, Rafferty went to work to face whatever the day brought.

Llewellyn had some good news for him for a change. The

roadside survey team had finally produced some results. A male driver had seen a Vauxhall Vectra drive down the Staveleys' road. He'd noticed it because the driver had annoyed him by taking such a time to make the right turn.

'That's great,' said Rafferty. 'What's this witness's name and where can we find him? Did he notice if the driver was a man or a woman?'

'He thought it was a woman, though he only saw her from the back. And the name of the man who saw the Vectra is Victor Pemberton. He lives here in Elmhurst at number 17 Station Road.'

'Have you got a phone number for him?'

'Yes.'

'Give him a bell, Dafyd. See if he noticed anything else about the car or the driver. I don't suppose he made a note of the registration number?'

'No. Why would he?' Llewellyn picked up the phone and dialled, but Victor Pemberton could tell them nothing more.

'A woman,' mused Rafferty. 'That means either Mrs Staveley Senior or her daughter, Helen Ayling.'

'Not necessarily. It could be someone else entirely. This woman could have been visiting the neighbour.'

'You're right, of course. And now I think of it, neither lady drives a Vectra. I saw a Jag outside her daughter's.' He snorted. 'So much for our roadside survey. That's all they've got? This one woman?'

'That's all.'

'I suppose we'd better try to check her out. Get on to Staveley's neighbour, Sarah Jones, would you, Daff? See if she had a visitor on the afternoon or evening of the murder. If we can do nothing else, we can at least eliminate her. And while I think of it, make a note to check out Gary Oldfield's girlfriend, Diana Rexton. Now we know for certain that Oldfield was having an affair with Adrienne it's possible she killed Adrienne in a fit of jealousy after finding out about the affair. It's a long shot, but possible.' Diana Rexton hadn't struck him as the sort of woman to seek retribution against her lover. She seemed the forgiving sort. In fact, she seemed to him to be the kind of woman who would let Oldfield get away with murder. Maybe he ought to check his alibi again while he was at it? See if Diana Rexton alters her story at all.

'Mr Oldfield won't like us questioning his girlfriend when it'll mean his affair with Mrs Staveley coming out. Miss Rexton is likely to want to know why we're pursuing him when she's already provided him with an alibi.'

'Too bad. I can't concern myself with his domestic difficulties. He should learn to keep his dick in his trousers. We'll go and see her this evening.'

Llewellyn turned to the telephone and Rafferty sat back and sipped the tea Llewellyn always fetched first thing. It was lukewarm, but sweet and strong, just as he liked it.

While Llewellyn was on the phone to Sarah Jones, Rafferty reflected on the case. He was disappointed that they had yet to find a firm lead. What if it wasn't one of their current crop of suspects who had killed Adrienne? What if it was someone else entirely? Someone who didn't even feature on their list? Such a thought was the stuff of nightmares; he could only hope it didn't give him another sleepless night.

Llewellyn came off the phone then and told Rafferty, 'Mrs Jones didn't have a visitor on the day of the murder.'

'Really? That's a turn up. There are only two houses down the Staveleys' side road, so this woman must have been visiting their house. Get back on to Sarah Jones and find out if she knows who drives a Vectra. If this woman is a regular visitor, she might know her.'

But unfortunately for Rafferty's turn of optimism, Sarah Jones wouldn't have recognized a Vauxhall Vectra if one ran her over. She knew nothing about the car or the driver, as Llewellyn discovered.

'Damn,' said Rafferty. 'I thought things were looking too rosy. Oh well, back to the drawing board.' Rafferty twiddled his thumbs while he thought of what to do next. 'Get on to John Staveley and see if he recognizes the car; maybe if this woman was a regular visitor to Adrienne, he'll know her.'

Llewellyn turned again to the phone, checked Staveley's telephone number and punched it in. The conversation didn't last long.

'He doesn't know anyone who drives a Vectra, either,' Llewellyn reported as he replaced the receiver.

Rafferty sighed. All their long shots were going down the pan. All they had left was Oldfield's girlfriend and he didn't

hold out much hope of anything coming from the next interview they had with her. They were seeing her this evening
and had agreed that, even if she didn't ask why they were
still questioning her about Oldfield's alibi, they would liven
things up with revelations about Oldfield's affair with Adrienne
Staveley. It was always interesting to stir the brew and see
what happened.

The afternoon wore desultorily away. Rafferty felt as if he
had been investigating this case for months. For some reason,
the plenitude of suspects fatigued his mind rather than ener-
gized it. Perhaps, after twenty odd years of going after assorted
murderers and other criminals, he was getting jaded. He
wouldn't be the first police officer to go down that road. It
was an occupational hazard. He'd known a few coppers, weary
of the chase, who had only hung on because the pension rights
were so good. Bill Beard was one of these, he'd been glad
enough to relinquish the murder hunts to the frisky youngsters coming up on his heels and retire – owing to his bad
back and varicose veins – to a job behind the reception desk.
Not that he'd ever struck Rafferty as being remotely ambi-
tious, having never aspired to rise above the rank of constable.

But, Rafferty told himself, you're an inspector in the CID
and supposedly in charge of catching this killer. No matter
how much he might sometimes long for it, he couldn't see
Bradley agreeing to him taking on the ease of desk duty.

Certainly not if Bradley thought it was what he wanted.
The superintendent had never liked him, but that dislike had
been confirmed when Rafferty had been unwise enough to
give into the impulse to take a rise out of Bradley. Oh well,
he thought, even as he cursed the impetuous Irishmen who
were his ancestors, there'll be no escape to a desk job for me
this side of retirement age.

That being the case, he'd better apply himself and try to
catch Adrienne Staveley's murderer.

And seeing as Rafferty was going to give Diana Rexton
the glad tidings of Oldfield's affair and probably break her
heart, he placated his stirring conscience with the thought that
at least it would lay bare the true nature of Oldfield's love,
which Rafferty felt he had guessed correctly was love for her
and her family's money rather than herself.

There had been no more reported sightings of Adrienne

Staveley with any other man and they had still to identify the third, mysterious man in her life. Rafferty, who still nursed hopes of proving that, somehow, Gary Oldfield was their killer, was glad to pack up and head over to Hidecote Manor that evening.

But when he got there, the odd-job man/father that again opened the door, told them that Diana wasn't there.

'She's gone back to the flat she shares with that bounder, Oldfield. Silly girl. I thought she had more sense. She should have, given her lack of good looks. Her sister's got beauty *and* brains.'

'I take it you don't like Gary Oldfield, sir. Can you tell me why?'

'Feller's a bounder, I told you. He's only after our Diana for her money – her grandmother left her a tidy sum and she's frittering it away buying him presents. Every time he comes here he's wearing some new expensive gewgaw or other. I thought she'd remain on the shelf and would look after her mother and me in our dotage. But no. Seems she intends devoting her life to looking after that fortune hunter.'

This last was obviously a sore point with Mr Rexton; clearly the thought of expensive care homes didn't appeal.

But Rafferty, preparing to break the news to Diana Rexton that her boyfriend was unfaithful, didn't have the patience to spare for this selfish old goat and he bade him a hasty goodbye and hurried back to the car.

'I'll drive,' he told Llewellyn, who had made for the driver's side of the car. 'I want to get to Oldfield's flat this evening rather than tomorrow.'

'More haste less speed. Surely there's no rush? We have all evening.'

'For all we know they're going out to cement their reconciliation.'

'If they're having a reconciliation. We don't know that they are.'

'We don't know that tomorrow's going to dawn, but it's likely.' To forestall any other delaying tactics, he got in the car, turned the ignition on and revved up. He was amused to see the rarely hurried Welshman yank open the passenger side door and fall into the seat. Llewellyn looked pained. He didn't like his dignity to be ruffled.

Although Rafferty felt bad about breaking what must be extremely unwelcome news, he was curious to see how Diana Rexton took it. He expected tears.

So when they got to the flat, he was surprised to find, when he told her of Oldfield's and Adrienne Staveley's affair, that she already knew. Or at least suspected.

Oldfield wasn't at home, unfortunately; Rafferty would have liked to drop his bombshell with him there to see the shock waves and their interaction. Denied this satisfaction, he contented himself with watching Diana Rexton's reaction.

She had been surprised to see them again and had clearly thought her evidence had exonerated her boyfriend of any suspicion of being mixed up with murder. Rafferty, sure that Oldfield had somehow tricked her into believing he hadn't left the flat that afternoon, felt sorry to disillusion her.

'Your father told us you'd come back here.'

'Did he?' She pulled a face. 'I found I couldn't stay there any longer. Daddy is rather horrid about Gary. He calls him a fortune hunter. He's not. He had no idea that my grandmother had left me some money when he first asked me out. He only realized I had money of my own when I bought a new Land Rover.'

Rafferty doubted that. He thought it probable that Oldfield had asked around at the tennis club and found out that the plain and probably grateful Diana Rexton came from a monied family.

She seemed to think her choice of vehicle merited some explanation, for she added, 'I often have to take a horse to events and the Land Rover is good and strong and excellent at getting out of muddy fields.'

She gazed placidly at him through her bottle-top spectacle lenses. She hadn't been wearing them the first time they had seen her: she'd probably taken them off in case her beloved Benjy got even more frisky than usual and broke them. They didn't improve her looks.

Rafferty braced himself and said to her, 'Perhaps your father's got a point. Your Gary was having an affair with Adrienne Staveley. Did you know?'

Diana Rexton's pallid face showed a crimson tide rising up from her neck. 'Oh,' she said. 'I didn't realize you knew. It's rather embarrassing.' She pleated her tweed skirt between her thick fingers.

Somehow Rafferty wasn't surprised that she knew already. He had half-suspected the reason she had gone to her parents' was because she and Gary had had a row. And that the row had been over Adrienne Staveley. Rafferty felt sorry for her. What was a nice girl like her doing getting mixed up with Gary Oldfield? Oldfield had said they hoped to marry. He thought it was likely to be a tragedy for her if they did so. Poor Diana – whose namesake, the late Princess of Wales, had been the epitome of style and beauty – didn't share the latter's looks or fashion sense. This Diana was a rather dowdy dresser and if she was bulimic there was no sign of it. Her waist was thick and her backside on the large side, something that her choice of jodhpurs as daily wear only emphasized.

'How did you find out?' he now asked her.

'A friend saw her and Gary together in a local pub. She followed them and told me they had been unable to keep their hands off one another. At first I gave Gary the benefit of the doubt, but later, when there would often be occasions he wasn't at the car lot and wasn't answering his mobile, I began to think that my friend had been right.'

Uncertainly, she said, 'I . . . I'd be grateful if you said nothing to Gary. He doesn't know I'm aware of their affair. He . . . he wouldn't like it. I wouldn't want him to think me deceitful.'

He could talk, thought Rafferty. In his opinion, Oldfield was scarcely in a position to find fault about the deception of others. He was careful to make no promises about not speaking to Gary Oldfield. 'So you didn't tackle him at all?'

She shook her head and said sadly, 'He'd only have denied it. The same way he denied that he still smoked and said it was his customers that came into the Portakabin with cigarettes that made his clothes reek of tobacco smoke. I believed him about that until I decided to surprise him one day and pop in to take him out to lunch.'

So she knew Oldfield was a liar. How much more disillusion would she stomach before she exorcised him from her life and bed? 'You're still happy to alibi him?'

'Oh yes,' she said. 'Gary might be guilty of many things, but murder isn't one of them. I know he didn't kill that woman. He was here from four o'clock onwards. He didn't leave the flat at all that afternoon or evening. I know because I was with him.'

Disgruntled that – although he felt sorry for her – he hadn't got a more satisfying reaction to his news, Rafferty left. He let Llewellyn drive. His only consolation being the fact that Oldfield was still unaware that his girlfriend knew about his affair. That suited Rafferty just fine. He looked forward to speaking to Mr Oldfield in the morning and letting him know that his faithless behaviour had been rumbled. But, as for the murder investigation, it would have to be a case of onward and upward. Onward and upward after the suspects who *were* still in the frame.

SEVEN

When Rafferty got home, it was to find Abra cock-a-hoop.

'I rang my young cousin today and she was delighted to be asked to be a bridesmaid,' she told Rafferty before he had even had a chance to get his jacket off.

'That's great, sweetheart. So all that worry was for nothing.'

'Yes. She's already been to the bridal wear shop and tried the dress on. It hardly needs any alteration.'

'Even better – less expense.' Whoops, he thought as soon as the words were out of his mouth. Not a good move.

'You're not going to start harping on about the cost of it all again, I hope.'

'No, my love,' Rafferty was quick to say, annoyed with himself that he'd let the comment slip. 'Nothing could be further from my thoughts.' They had already split up once over what Abra called his cheapskate attitude to the rising costs of the wedding. They'd managed to get over that and Rafferty was determined that the subject wasn't going to come between them again.

'I hope you're hungry,' said Abra. 'I've made a casserole with dumplings.'

'Dumplings. Mmm. I love dumplings.'

'You love anything that's called food.' Abra laughed. 'You're the original dustbin.'

'Call me what you like. But you can't say I don't appreciate your cooking.'

'True. I'll go and dish up. Come into the kitchen and tell me about your day.'

Rafferty followed Abra through into the kitchen. He ate one of the dished out dumplings and Abra gave him a slap.

'Wait, greedy guts. That's one less for you.'

'Worth it though. Tastes lovely.'

'Should do. I've slaved over it.'

'What did I do to deserve you? I must have been a good boy in a previous life.'

'You want to concentrate on being a good boy in *this* one.'

'I will. Promise.'

'So how's your murder coming along? Are you any closer to arresting someone?'

'Not yet, though I'm seriously tempted – even if it's just to get the superintendent off my back.'

'So, he's still the great support he's always been?'

'You could say that. He thinks by hectoring his officers he pushes them on to solving their cases. The reality, of course, is something else. A superintendent who spends his time with one eye on Region isn't going to be in your corner when needed.'

'Bosses, hey? There's more bad ones about than ever these days. No wonder cases of stress in the workplace are rising.'

'Talking of stress in the workplace – how's your strike threat coming on?'

'It's still just a possibility, though a couple of the secretaries are muttering about it loud enough for the head honcho to hear. They'll get their marching orders if they're not careful. One of them's still on her probation period, so won't have any employment protection and the other one's a contract worker, so I don't know where she'd stand.'

'I think you should be thankful you've still got a job and that your firm's a profitable one. There are too many people on the dole and scrabbling for work these days to risk losing secure employment.'

'Oh pooh. I can hear your mother talking. She was always one for security at any cost. You can't blame her I suppose as she was widowed so young. It'd make anyone cautious. And even though you were widowed young, too, you were hardly in the same position as your mother to so harp on about security. Anyone would think you didn't want me to be a kept woman. But don't worry. I don't want to be a kept woman, either. I've always enjoyed having financial independence and I won't give it up when we marry.'

'I haven't asked you to.'

'No. And you won't. You want to keep me working, you slave driver.'

'Well, as that's what you want to do I can't see what the problem is.'

'Do you know something? Neither can I. Let's get dinner.'

Abra brought the plates through to the living room and
Rafferty tucked in heartily. 'This is great,' he said. 'You can
do this again. It really hits the spot.'

'Good. I aim to please. So I'll see a clean plate?'

'You bet. Mind I don't start on yours after.'

'You dare.'

They ate in silence for a couple of minutes then Rafferty
said, 'You've heard about my day tell me about yours.'

'Busy. Adrian Gallagher sent in his note. It put my boss in
a foul mood.'

Adrian Gallagher, as Rafferty recollected from previous
work chats, was one of her theatrical agency's star turns and
most difficult clients. He was demanding and never satisfied.

Today, it seemed, he had written to say he was moving
himself and his high earning capacity to another agency. No
wonder, on top of the simmering strike threat, it had put her
boss in a bad mood.

'Anyway, I told them I had a dental appointment and finished
early, which is why I had time to make a casserole.'

'All I can say is finish early again.'

'I'll have to have a word with my boss and tell him my
husband-to-be demands his dumplings so I have to finish early
regularly.'

'Do that.'

'As if. I'll get the sack and you'll be able to have dumplings
every day.'

'Suits me.'

'Well it doesn't suit me. I'd be bored out of my skull if I
was at home every day.'

'Still, you might have to think about it if we have a baby.'

'I'll think about it when that happens. So how many kids
do you want, anyway?'

'Four seems a nice round number.'

'Four? That's two too many for me. My name might mean
"Mother of multitudes", but that doesn't mean I have to live
up to it. After all it won't be you that has to have them.'

'True. But I'll help with feeds and nappies. As the oldest
of six I've plenty of practice with nappies.'

'That's good to know. Still let's get the wedding over first
before we start thinking of tiny feet pattering.'

'Talking of the wedding, have you got your dress yet?'

'Yes. Of course. You don't think I'd leave it till the last minute, do you? It's in the wardrobe at my flat.'

'What's it like?'

'I'm not telling you. You'll find out soon enough.'

'I'll bet you look gorgeous in it.'

'You bet right. I do.'

'I knew you would. I don't look so bad myself in my wedding gear.'

'We'll make a perfect pair then.'

'Won't we just? I can't wait. These last days till we get hitched seem to be taking forever. I can't wait to be married to you. It can't come quickly enough for me.'

'You always have to wait for the best things in life,' Abra teased him. 'Meanwhile you can help me stack the dishwasher.'

'I'll do it. You pour us both a drink and sit down. After preparing and cooking such a lovely meal you deserve a break from being a domestic goddess.'

This was something of a joke, because Abra would be the first one to admit she hated housework.

Abra smiled. 'I do love a volunteer.'

'I'll volunteer to do anything for you.'

'Good. Get clearing then.'

'Yes, Mam.' Rafferty picked up the plates and headed for the kitchen. It didn't take long to stack the dishwasher and he was soon back. He sat down on the settee and raised his glass. 'Cheers. Here's to our wedding day and our future together.'

'Seconded. To tell the truth I can't wait either.'

Rafferty got up and put a CD on the stereo. 'I thought we'd have a bit of music. I've put Barry White on. I know he's one of your favourite singers.'

'Thanks, love. Come and sit down.'

Rafferty lowered himself on to the settee next to Abra, picked up his glass and took a sip. 'That hits the spot. It's been a rough day. I've all these suspects and nothing certain about any of them.' Apart from one, he said to himself. And the certain thing I have about *him*, I'd rather not have.

'Poor Joe. Are there no leads?'

'Not so's you'd notice. And few alibis. There are a number of suspects who could be guilty of the murder but no proof against any of them.'

'You'll get there. You always have before.'

'Sometimes more by luck than judgement.'

'It doesn't matter how you get there as long as you do.'

'I suppose so. I'll have to hope for a bit of luck on this one I think.'

'Say some prayers then. Get in practice for the wedding.'

'Say some prayers? I've had enough of prayers. Father Kelly's been putting me through my paces these last few weeks. You'd think it might have earned me some brownie points with the Almighty and led him to put some luck my way, but it hasn't.'

'Never mind. Come to bed. Barry White's got me all tingly. Perhaps a bit of physical activity will make you feel better.'

'Perhaps it will. I'm prepared to give it a try.'

'Thought you might be.' Abra laughed. She finished her drink and stood up. 'Come on then, lover. Let's go and make beautiful Barry White music together.'

Rafferty knocked back the rest of his Jameson's and stood up with alacrity. 'Anything you say, Mam. After you in the bathroom.'

Abra led the way. The bathroom ablutions didn't take long and they were soon tucked up cosily in bed.

Rafferty put his arm around Abra and kissed her. 'Just think – soon you'll be Mrs Rafferty. I can't wait to make an honest woman of you.'

'I'm an honest woman already, I'll have you know, Joseph Aloysius.'

'Not that name again, I beg you.'

'Kiss me again and I'll think about it.'

Rafferty duly obliged, then asked, 'Are you thinking?'

'You bet, Ally.'

'Think a bit harder.'

'I'd rather get down and dirty.'

'Me too. But you can still do some thinking while we make beautiful music together.'

'Let's hear the music first and I'll see.'

Rafferty, used to obeying orders, duly obliged.

Rafferty had slept well. He got up, eager to speak to Gary Oldfield. The man had already proved himself a liar; maybe he had persuaded Diana Rexton to lie for him also. Because, in spite of her transparent honesty, it was clear she was head over heels in love with Oldfield and would do anything for him, even connive in the cover-up of murder. He was looking forward to breaking the news that his grubby little secret was secret no longer. It didn't take long, once breakfasted, for him to pick up Llewellyn and get over there.

'Why did you have to tell Diana about me and Adrienne? Now she'll want me to tell her every five minutes that I love her. I could have done without you upsetting her.'

'I rather think it's *you* that has upset your girlfriend, sir. She said she already knew about the affair before we brought the matter up.'

'She can't have. How?'

Rafferty explained that one of Diana's friends had seen him with Adrienne Staveley.

Oldfield scowled. 'Some nosy old biddy, I expect. With nothing better to do.' His next words showed that he was keen to implicate someone other than himself. 'If you think me a suspect, you should check out Adrienne's brother-in-law. He had the hots for her and visited her a couple of times a week, but she wasn't interested.'

'And how do you know he had the hots for her, as you call it?'

'Because Adrienne told me. She thought it was funny and was considering encouraging him in order to cock a snook at Helen, her sister-in-law.'

'Why would she want to do that?'

'Helen Ayling didn't approve of her. She thinks the sun shines out of her husband's backside and is extremely jealous whenever another woman flirts with him.'

'I see. Well thank you for that information, sir. We'll check it out.'

'Do that. I know you think Diana is lying for me, but she isn't. I didn't kill Adrienne. I didn't leave the flat from the time I came home from work to the time I went to bed.'

'So you say, sir. But I'm not sure I believe you. And then there's the matter of Adrienne pushing you to live with her. That must have caused some friction. Weren't you worried that Adrienne would make it her business to tell your girlfriend what you and she were up to?'

'No way. Adrienne wouldn't do that.'

'Again, we've only got your word for that. I get the impression that Adrienne Staveley was a woman who liked her own way. I don't believe she would have taken your refusal with any understanding. In fact, I don't find it hard to imagine her losing her temper about it.'

'Well, she didn't. She didn't really want us to set up home together. Apart from anything else, she's got a terrific home. What would she get with me but a miserable poky flat much like the one I share with Diana?'

'Maybe she thought you were worth the sacrifice, sir,' Rafferty mischievously suggested.

'Well, that went well,' Rafferty commented once he and Llewellyn were back in the car. 'Now we have two more suspects to add to the list. Just what we needed.' Rafferty decided to see David Ayling in his office immediately after seeing Oldfield and he got the phone number of Ayling's wife from Llewellyn in order to get the address.

David Ayling's office was in the centre of Elmhurst in a medieval building that looked unsuitable for twenty-first-century technology.

Ayling greeted them nicely enough, but when Rafferty broached the reason for their visit he clammed up and was only reluctantly persuaded to open up a little.

'It's true, I got on with Adrienne very well,' he finally admitted.

'I've been told you liked her more than was wise for a married man.'

David Ayling, who seemed a shy, retiring man, blushed. 'I liked Adrienne. She was an exciting woman and as you said, I'm an old married man.'

'Were you in love with her?' Rafferty asked.

'Love? What's that? I fancied her. I don't know if that would be considered being in love.'

'I understand you were in the habit of visiting Mrs Staveley at her home after work.'

Ayling blushed again. 'I liked to see her. She welcomed my visits.'

'And did your wife know about them?'

'I don't believe so. I saw no reason to mention them.'

I bet you didn't, was Rafferty's thought.

Ayling ran his hand over his balding head. He was tall,

skinny and had a middle-aged paunch. Rafferty found it hard
to believe that Adrienne Staveley would have been attracted to
him. Had she laughed in his face and angered him? That could
be enough to get her murdered.

'You said Mrs Staveley welcomed your visits. How did this
welcome manifest itself?'

'She invited me into her living room and offered me drinks.

'Did she flirt with you?'

'I suppose so. I was flattered. She was an attractive woman.
I'd have stayed there all evening if I could, but John Staveley
always came home around six, six thirty. I left before then,
as he wouldn't have liked to find me there.'

'Why not? You're her brother-in-law, after all.'

'John didn't like Adrienne having men friends.'

'Even if they were family?'

'Even if they were family. They didn't socialize with us.
If John wanted to see Helen, he'd arrange to meet her in town.
I scarcely saw anything of him.'

'How often did you drop in on Mrs Staveley?'

'A couple of times a week.'

'What did you tell your wife when you were late home?'

'I didn't tell her anything. I imagine she just assumed I was
working late. I often do.'

'I see. Did you see Adrienne on the day she was murdered?'

'No.' Ayling was quick to deny it.

'So where were you between four and six on that day?'

'I was here. I really was working late.'

'And can anyone confirm that?'

'No. Not after five thirty. I was here alone then.'

Time enough for him to drive to Adrienne's home, try to
kiss her, be rebuffed and strangle her. Ayling sounded as if
he had been obsessive about the dead woman. Almost a stalker
and there had been enough cases of stalkers killing the object
of their obsession.

But yet again, they could have all the suspicions they liked,
but without proof . . .

Abruptly, Rafferty told him, 'Thanks for being so frank.
We'll leave you to get on with your work.'

Once in the car, Rafferty and Llewellyn discussed the interview. 'Think he did it?' Rafferty asked.

'It's possible. He may have been aware that Mrs Staveley

laughed at him. Her manner towards him might have shown her opinion of him.'

'Mmm. No man likes being laughed at, particularly by a woman they find sexually attractive. He's yet another suspect. Pity. I was hoping to whittle them down a bit by now. Certainly, by more than Gary Oldfield.'

'Another suspect and another possibility,' Llewellyn commented as he turned the key in the ignition.

'There's always that, I suppose.' Rafferty hadn't looked at it that way. 'Then there's Helen Ayling. She could be another suspect if she's the jealous type as Gary Oldfield said and if she learned of her husband's visits to Adrienne.'

As for Adrienne's second lover, Peacock, he didn't think the clearly besotted Peacock capable of killing an Adrienne he clearly adored. Of course, Helen Ayling's husband, David, had been as besotted as Peacock – there was certainly enough passion there for violence – and it seemed a much hotter passion than Peacock's, too. *Had* Adrienne encouraged David Ayling when he had tried to take her flirting further? Rafferty could imagine Ayling killing her in the white heat of rage if she rejected him after toying with his affections. And he had no alibi. But then neither did John Staveley or his son.

Rafferty realized he'd come full circle, but had advanced the investigation not one jot. He sighed. 'Oh well, Bradley, for one, will be pleased. And at least it means I've got something to tell him for once. Come on,' he said, 'put your foot down and let's get back to the station. I'm sure Bradley's hopping up and down waiting for me to put in an appearance. I'd hate to disappoint him.'

EIGHT

The next morning the mystery, third, man in Adrienne Staveley's life turned up at the station. Rafferty was surprised when Bill Beard on reception rang through to tell him of Richard Simpson's arrival. Simpson had certainly taken his time in coming forward. He wondered what had prompted him to do so now.

Simpson was in his early thirties and when Rafferty collected him from reception and brought him back to his office, he categorically denied that he had been Adrienne's lover.

'We were just friends,' he insisted. 'I only met her a few weeks ago. There wasn't time for the relationship to develop beyond friendship.'

Time enough for most people, Rafferty thought, in this modern age. And given that Adrienne had bedded Michael Peacock on the day she had met him . . . 'Did you go to her house?' he asked.

'Yes. A couple of times. Just to pick her up for lunch. There was no hanky panky.'

'When did you last see her?'

'A week before she died. I took her to lunch and dropped her home after. I didn't go in.'

'Have you ever been in her kitchen? I'm thinking about fingerprints.'

'No. The only rooms I've been in are the hall and the lounge and I didn't spend much time in either – just long enough for Adrienne to put on her jacket and pick up her handbag.'

'We'll need to take your prints just to be sure. I'll arrange for an officer to take them, after we've finished, if that's convenient.'

Simpson nodded assent.

'Tell me, Mr Simpson, where were you on the afternoon and early evening on the day of the murder?'

'You want an alibi I take it?'

Rafferty nodded. 'If you'd be so good.'

'Let me see. I was in Chelmsford all morning for a meeting.

I had lunch there. Then I drove back and reached my office here in Elmhurst about two o'clock. I was there for the rest of the day till about five o'clock.'

So he'd still have had time to murder Adrienne supposing she died at the latter stage of Dally's estimate. Of course, Simpson might have left his office and killed her earlier in the afternoon.

'And where did you go after you left work?'

'I went home.'

'And your address is?'

Simpson told him and Llewellyn made a note of it.

'Is there anyone at home who can vouch for you after five?'

'I'm afraid not. Not unless my neighbour saw me arrive or heard me shut my front door.'

'We'll need your business address also, sir.'

Llewellyn made a note of that as well.

Still curious as to why Simpson had chosen to come forward now, he questioned the man about it.

Simpson fiddled with his gold earring and admitted, 'I nearly didn't. But, from the description in the paper, I assumed I was the mystery third man in her life that the local newspaper referred to and I finally concluded that it would be better for me to admit to being that third man than have you trace me. If I hadn't come forward it would have made me all the more suspect.'

'I see. Well, thank you for coming into the station, Mr Simpson. I appreciate that and your frankness.' Rafferty then told him he could go as soon as Llewellyn had escorted him to have his prints taken.

'We'll need to check out what he says,' said Rafferty fifteen minutes later, on Llewellyn's return. 'Let's get over to his office and make sure he was there when he said he was. Then we'll try his neighbours and see if any of them saw him arrive home.'

Simpson's office alibi checked out, at least at first glance. But a second glance revealed a fire escape leading down from his office and a secretary who had been absent from the office from four thirty on the afternoon of the murder to attend a dental appointment. He had no alibi to confirm what time he reached home, either. None of his neighbours had seen his car drive up and park and his closest neighbour hadn't heard his front door shut, so Simpson was yet another possible suspect. Rafferty couldn't help but wonder when the wretched list would stop growing.

Rafferty said as much as he and Llewellyn made their way back to the car after checking out Simpson's neighbours.

'But possibly a less likely suspect given that he's only known the victim for a few weeks.'

'So he says. We've no way of proving it one way or the other. Besides Adrienne Staveley seems to have been the sort of woman to attract violent emotions. Maybe just a few weeks would be long enough to make someone want to throttle her.'

'We know she didn't get on with her husband, his family or her stepson, but she seems to have got on well enough with the other men in her life.'

'Unless she had a falling out with one of them.' Rafferty ran his hand through his already disordered auburn hair. 'And it strikes me as unlikely that her relationship with Richard Simpson would remain at a mere friendship level. The other two men in her life that we know about both became her lovers, one of them on the day of meeting – why would she wait to make Simpson the third – or thirty-third for all we know?'

'Maybe she didn't and Simpson's lying. He wouldn't be the first suspect to lie to us in a murder inquiry.'

'Ain't that the truth. Oh well, we're not going to find answers to that or anything else from sitting here on our arses.' Rafferty fastened his seatbelt. 'Let's get back to the station. I'll get on the blower on the way and get Gerry Hanks to put Simpson through the computer to check him out. Maybe he's got a history of violent attacks on women.'

However, the answer to this question came back in the negative.

'Doesn't necessarily mean anything,' Rafferty said as they drew up at the traffic lights near the police station. 'Every murderer has to start somewhere.'

'True, but usually they've shown signs of violence earlier.'

'Maybe he did but we just didn't catch him. Anyway, usually isn't always. And none of the men in this case has a criminal record. Could be she just goaded one of them beyond endurance. I mean look at her poor husband, who chooses to walk the streets all day rather than go home to his wife.

Look at the stepson who spends time after school at the library, studying, when he could work just as well at home. Our victim seems to have caused extreme reactions, at least amongst the men in her life. It's the sort of behaviour liable to get a woman killed. I'm inclined to think that's what happened in this case.'

They arrived back at the station. The morning dragged into lunchtime, then afternoon. They ate canteen sandwiches at their desks and studied more reports.

The phone broke the drowsy stillness of the post-noon hour. Rafferty picked it up. 'DI Rafferty. Oh, hello, Mr Staveley,' he said. 'He's what? When? Yesterday? And you're only reporting it now?' Rafferty listened for a few more seconds, then said, 'We'll be over directly,' and put the phone down.

'Guess what,' he said to Llewellyn. 'That was John Staveley. His son's gone missing. Run away, it sounds like. Guilty conscience, do you think?'

'Maybe he's just overwrought. You know what teenagers are like with their topsy-turvy emotions.'

'Mmm, maybe so. Anyway I said we'd go over there. There's not a lot else happening, God knows.' They put on their jackets and walked downstairs and out to the car park.

When they got to John Staveley's house, he appeared distraught – far more so than he had seemed after his wife's murder. Was this another possible pointer to guilt, along with the fact that he and his wife hadn't been getting on?

Staveley invited them into his living room and they all sat down. Llewellyn took out his notebook. Staveley ran his hands through his hair and said, 'You've got to find him. I'm going out of my mind with worry. Kyle's not a streetwise boy. Anything could happen to him.'

'All right, Mr Staveley. Calm down. Tell me what you know.'

'He left for school as usual yesterday morning on his bike, with his school bag, but he never got there. I rang a couple of Kyle's friends when he didn't come home and they told me as much.'

'I see. Was he wearing his school uniform?'

'Yes, of course. I'd have noticed if he hadn't been.'

'Have you any idea where he might have gone?'

Staveley ran his hands through his hair again. By now, it

was standing on end, and he shook his head. 'I've rung everyone I can think of, but no one's seen him. He could be anywhere. Anything could happen to him.'

'Did he take any clothes with him?'

'I suppose he must have. His schoolbooks are in his bedroom. He must have emptied them out of his bag and used it for his clothes. But I don't know what he's taken. He's got a lot of stuff.'

'OK, sir. Could you let me have a recent photo of Kyle?'

'Yes. I've got his latest school photo. It's on the mantelpiece. I'll get it.'

He stood up and walked over to the fireplace, removed the photo from the frame and handed it to Rafferty. 'I'd like it back.'

'Of course. We'll copy it and return it to you as soon as possible. While we're here, we'll need to see his bedroom.'

'His bedroom? Why?'

'There may be something that will give us a clue to his whereabouts,' Rafferty explained.

'I see. Yes, of course. Whatever will help. It's first left at the top of the stairs.'

Rafferty and Llewellyn climbed to the first floor and entered Kyle's bedroom. It was the usual teenage pit of disorder, with drawers pulled out and clothes and other belongings strewn about. It was difficult to know where to start.

Rafferty began with the drawers of the dresser but all it contained was jumpers and underwear. Next, he looked under the pillows and mattress, but there was nothing hidden under either. He took off the pillowcases, but all they contained were pillows. The wardrobe came next. He hunted through the pockets of jackets, anoraks and trousers and came up with nothing but fluff, used tissues and pieces of string. There wasn't a clue to Kyle's whereabouts anywhere in the room, so they returned downstairs.

'I'd like to talk to Kyle's friends, Mr Staveley,' Rafferty told him. 'So if you could let me have their names and addresses . . . I presume they attend the same school as your son?'

'Yes. Elmhurst Comprehensive. Their names are Jason Endecott and Andrew Prendergast.' He supplied their home addresses and Llewellyn noted the details down. 'He had other

friends, friends he had made at his private school, but he
doesn't see them now. I think he's ashamed to mix with them
now he's going to the comprehensive.'

Rafferty gave a sympathetic nod. 'You didn't tell me why
you left it so late to tell us about Kyle's disappearance.'

Staveley rubbed an unsteady hand over his unshaven face
and slumped further back into his armchair. 'I . . . I suppose
I was worried that it looked bad for Kyle. I thought you'd
think he ran away because he was guilty. But he's never been
close to sudden death before. Neither have I for that matter.
He's just a boy. A frightened boy.'

Maybe he was, thought Rafferty but he chose to run away
at a particularly pertinent time. It wasn't necessarily a pointer
to guilt – of course it wasn't. And maybe Kyle was just a
crazy, mixed up kid, but when they found him – if they found
him – he would have a few questions to answer.

There was clearly nothing else to be learned here though.
John Staveley couldn't even tell them which of Kyle's clothes
were missing and the boy's bedroom had told them nothing.
Maybe his friends, when questioned, would admit to knowing
more than they'd told Kyle's father.

They drove over to where Jason Endecott lived. Luckily,
the boy was in, as his mother confirmed. Rafferty told her
why he wanted to question her son and she led them up to
Jason's bedroom where he was working on his computer. Not
that he could tell them any more than he'd told Staveley.

'You're sure Kyle didn't say anything to you?' Rafferty
questioned.

'Of course I'm sure. I'd tell you if I knew anything. Kyle
said nothing to me, nothing at all.'

'OK, Jason.' Rafferty produced a card and handed it to the
boy. 'But if you remember anything, please give me a ring.'

Jason nodded and shoved Rafferty's card in his pocket. Mrs
Endecott apologized for the fact that her son couldn't be more
helpful and showed them out.

'Let's get over to Kyle's other friend, Andrew Prendergast,'
Rafferty said when she shut the front door behind them.
'Maybe he knows more.'

But they were doomed to disappointment there, too, as
Andrew Prendergast could tell them no more than Jason.

They went back to the station and Rafferty got Llewellyn

to arrange for Kyle's photo to be copied and sent to the media. He issued a statement to go with it. At a guess, he assumed that Kyle would have made for London. It was where most runaways headed. He sent officers to the local train station to see if Kyle had been spotted there boarding a train to London. He also sent officers to the bus station to question the staff there and despatched a copy of Kyle's photo to one of his contacts in the Met for circulation. Kyle had, according to his father, set off on his bike in his school uniform. But presumably, he would quickly have changed out of that as Elmhurst Comprehensive's maroon blazer was pretty distinctive. Kyle would want to make himself as anonymous as possible. And then there was the bike; had he taken it wherever he'd gone? Or had he dumped it somewhere? After ringing John Staveley and getting a description of the bike, he dispatched more officers to check the routes out of town that Kyle might have taken if he'd decided to hitch a ride and dump the bike. He'd covered every eventuality now, all he could do was await results.

There was still no sighting of Kyle by the next morning. John Staveley rang every hour on the hour, seeking answers, but Rafferty had none to give him. In any case, they couldn't concentrate solely on Kyle Staveley, tempting as it might be. They still had other suspects, other possible motives to look into.

The fingerprints in the Staveleys' kitchen and the other rooms revealed a wealth of information. Those of two of Adrienne's male friends, Gary Oldfield and Michael Peacock, were much in evidence, as were those of the family and nearest neighbour, of course.

Rafferty was aghast to discover that Abra's fingerprints were found in the kitchen and other rooms. What had she been doing there? Had she known the dead woman? He was stunned also to find she had a criminal record for drug possession. He hadn't known she had a drug problem. He was so discombobulated that he barely heard Llewellyn's comments concerning the several prints that they were unable to identify. His answers were reflex ones, scarcely passing through his brain on their way to his lips.

'Perhaps they're from Kyle's friends,' Llewellyn suggested.

'I can't see him bringing his friends home to *that* house,'
Rafferty replied as he sat back in his chair and picked up his
cup, his mind a whirl of conflicting thoughts. 'He didn't like
spending time there himself, so he wouldn't want to subject
his friends to his stepmother's presumed lack of welcome. It's
my guess he would go to his friends' houses rather than the
reverse.'

Slowly, Llewellyn nodded. 'Mmm, you're probably right.
Still I think we should get their prints just to eliminate them.'

'Do that. And while you're organizing that, I'll go and break
the happy news of Kyle's disappearance to the super.' He'd
been trying to come up with a reason to put this off as he
knew the kind of reception the news would receive.

However, when no good excuse occurred to him, he said,
'Wish me luck, as it's not going to go down too well.'

Rafferty was right. Superintendent Bradley was not best
pleased: to hear him you'd think Rafferty had supplied Kyle
with his train fare himself.

'Surely the boy gave some indication of his intentions?'
Bradley questioned once Rafferty had sat down and broken
the bad news.

'Not to me he didn't. And his father seemed just as surprised
as I was. He wasn't even able to tell me which of the boy's
clothes were missing. He's been no help at all and neither
have Kyle's two school friends. He kept his plans very close
to his chest.'

'Well, find him, Rafferty. You've had his photo circulated
among the media at least?'

'Of course.' Stung by the implication of incompetence,
Rafferty's reply was brusque. He found himself staring
beyond the super to the wall behind him. The wall was a
testimonial to Bradley's monumental ego, covered as it was
with photos of him with various local and national worthies,
the broadest of grins on his fat face. Rafferty had never seen
him grin like that.

'I suppose that's something, but I'm not pleased with the
way this case is progressing – or should I say *not* progressing?
I want to see some movement and I want to see it soon. Do
you understand me?'

'Yes, sir,' was Rafferty's sullen reply.

'Get off then and get me some results. *Someone* must have

seen Mrs Staveley's killer. Someone must have seen this boy, this Kyle. It's up to you to find them. I want some results, Rafferty. I've got Region breathing down my neck on this one.'

Rafferty just stopped himself from slamming the door behind him. 'Bloody man,' he muttered to himself as he walked up the stairs. 'Why couldn't he get promoted to Region and out of my hair?'

'Talking to yourself young Rafferty? asked Bill Beard, the reception desk constable as he walked down the stairs towards him. 'They say that's the first sign of madness.'

'Who'd wonder at it? I've just been in to see the not-so-super and he chewed me out and then some. The man expects miracles and evidence produced out of thin air. Jesus Christ I ain't.'

'He's brass, me duck.' Beard was generous with his endearments, even when addressing senior officers. He was something of an institution at the station, having been there longer than anyone else. 'What can you expect?'

Rafferty shrugged. 'Nothing, I suppose.'

'Then you won't be disappointed, will you?'

Rafferty sniffed and made for his office, his mind in turmoil as he wondered how best to tackle Abra about her presence in the death house, not to mention how to conceal the fact of her presence there from the rest of the team.

He'd have to share this information with Llewellyn as he knew there was no way he could keep it from him. Besides, Abra was Dafyd's cousin, so Rafferty thought it only fair that he should share the burden of unwanted knowledge.

But what to do about it was down to him. He wished he had some notion of what action he might take.

NINE

Kyle Staveley had still not been found by the next day, in spite of all their efforts to trace him. If he had disappeared into London's vast maw, there was no telling when he'd be found. But meanwhile, the rest of the investigation was continuing. Not that that was going any better than the hunt for Kyle. No new leads had turned up and no new evidence against their current crop of suspects had been found. Rafferty didn't know what to do next to get the results the super was demanding. He'd done everything by the book, with no result worthy of the name. Despairing, he asked Llewellyn if he had any suggestions.

'Only one,' the Welshman replied. 'And that's to check all the CCTV footage along the most likely routes from our suspects' homes to the Staveleys' house to see if one of their cars shows up.'

Rafferty groaned. 'That'll take forever.'

'We've little enough else to work on. And it's not as if you have to do it yourself. At least we'd feel we were doing something constructive.'

'I suppose so. All right, Dafyd. Get it arranged, will you? It will give me something to tell the super so he doesn't think we've been completely idle.'

Llewellyn went out to do his bidding and Rafferty slumped back in his chair. He swung it round and gazed out of the window as though seeking inspiration in the mature sycamore trees opposite the station. It was a fine day: a glorious early summer day with blue skies and fluffy white clouds. Rafferty wished he were out in it instead of cooped up in his office, with thoughts of Abra's possible complicity in their latest murder case to keep him company. He hadn't been able to avoid telling Llewellyn that her prints had been found at the scene – in fact, her prints had been numerous and found in every room of the house which indicated an unwelcome intimacy with either John Staveley or Adrienne. He wasn't sure which one he would prefer it to be. If it was John Staveley it indicated an intimacy that Rafferty would rather not think about. Yet if it was Adrienne that Abra was intimate with it was even more worrying. He'd never heard Abra mention Adrienne's name, which indicated that it was John Staveley who had entertained her in his bedroom. He was worried sick that his fiancée was having an affair. Their wedding was only a few weeks away, for God's sake. How could he go through with it if she was cheating on him already? He felt sick and disenchanted, not remotely up to leading the team in the investigation.

Llewellyn had been sympathetic to his predicament, but had advised being honest with Abra. As usual with the Welshman, he had resorted to Latin:

'*Quidquid agas prudenter agas et respice finem*. Whatever you do, do with caution, and look to the end,' was Llewellyn's quick translation.

It hadn't helped.

But, if, by some miracle, it was *Adrienne* rather than John Staveley that she knew, at least the rest of the team didn't know that the Abra Anne Kearney who featured on the police computer was his fiancée. Those amongst the team who knew he was engaged thought his fiancée's name was Abby as that was how he generally referred to her when speaking of her at work. Although Llewellyn had suggested tackling her head on about why she'd been at the Staveleys' home, Rafferty wasn't keen on doing this. If she knew he had her listed as a possible murder suspect there was no knowing what she'd do. The same applied if he told her he suspected her of cheating on him. It wasn't so long since she'd come back after she'd left him over what she regarded as his cheeseparing attitude to the wedding. He didn't want to risk her flouncing out and back to her own flat again. It was a very delicate problem and no matter which way he looked at it he couldn't find a ready answer as to how to tackle it.

The only good thing was that Llewellyn had agreed it would be wise to keep Abra's presence in the murder house secret from the team. So in Rafferty's briefing and handing out of duties, he made sure not to mention her name. He would have to question her himself sometime and somehow, only not yet.

He longed for a cigarette, but he'd given up smoking, so didn't have any. To stop himself thinking about the Abra problem and his craving for a cigarette, he turned his mind back to the investigation. Not that that gave any comfort. Was there anything else they could do? He couldn't think of anything; they'd already covered all the angles and then some. All he could hope for was that Llewellyn's haul through the CCTV footage brought a result. And not one that involved Abra visiting the house during the four to six p.m. murder timeline.

In this, he was lucky and in a remarkably short time. Llewellyn and the other officers he'd set to the task of checking saw Gary Oldfield's car, rather than Abra's, on the last CCTV camera leading out of town, yet he'd said he'd been at home all afternoon on the day of Adrienne Staveley's murder. And so had his live-in girlfriend, Diana Rexton. Rafferty was keen to learn what he'd have to say for himself, so he and Llewellyn got themselves over to Oldfield's flat. He was glad of an excuse to get out in the sunshine. But neither Oldfield nor his girlfriend were in, so instead they headed for the used car lot where he was employed.

It was a short journey from Oldfield's flat to his place of work. Rafferty parked up outside the lot, then walked through the parked cars, all gleaming brightly in the sunshine. A young lad was busy polishing one of them. There were about thirty cars in the lot – all polished to a knock-your-eyes-out shimmer. Much like Gary Oldfield. It must be like painting the Forth Bridge was Rafferty's thought. And he didn't know which of the two would take longest to prettify up.

Oldfield was chatting to a customer, but Rafferty had no compunction about interrupting the conversation. As soon as he and Llewellyn flashed their IDs, the customer took off in a hurry. Must have a guilty conscience, Rafferty surmised. But he wasn't interested in pursuing some petty crook today, so the customer escaped any questioning.

Oldfield scowled at their approach. 'You've just lost me a sale,' he complained.

'Sorry about that, sir,' said Rafferty, not at all sorry. He didn't like Oldfield who he considered to be a smarmy git. 'But murder has to take precedence.' He paused, then said, 'We've unearthed some new evidence. You did say you were at home all afternoon and evening on the day of the murder, didn't you, sir?'

Oldfield's gaze shifted uneasily between them before he said, 'Yes. Yes I did. What of it?'

'Only we've discovered that's not true, sir.' Rafferty pulled out a still photo taken from the CCTV. 'That *is* your car, sir? You can see the registration clearly as well as the date and time. This particular camera is located on the way to the Staveleys' house and the still shows a time of five o'clock. So why did you lie to us?'

Oldfield's smooth face didn't change colour at his lie being found out. In fact, he looked remarkably at ease for a man caught out in an untruth in a murder investigation. Instead of answering, he turned and made for the Portakabin. They followed him and watched as Oldfield opened the metal key cabinet and replaced a set of car keys. Carefully, he locked it again before he turned back to face them and answered, 'I forgot. I went out to get a takeaway.'

'But you must have passed half a dozen takeaways between your flat and the last CCTV camera. What was wrong with them?'

'Like most people, I have my preferred takeaways. I just find the Chinese on the outskirts of town the best. They've had several good write-ups in the local press by the restaurant critic. They've even been praised by one of the nationals.'

'Is that so?' Rafferty was peeved. He knew he couldn't prove it either way. The CCTV footage showed Oldfield's car returning some fifteen minutes later; time enough to reach the Staveleys' house and kill Adrienne, though, equally, it would take about that amount of time, if he had been in the Chinese takeaway, to select, order and wait for his food. Trouble was, there was no CCTV camera by the Staveleys' home, or the Chinese takeaway, so he couldn't prove that Oldfield had gone to either place. 'So what's the name of the takeaway you used?'

'I can't remember its name, but it's on the corner of All Saints' Avenue.'

'And how did you pay?'

Oldfield smiled. 'By cash. Sorry. It means I can't prove I was there.'

Rafferty silently cursed. It also meant that he couldn't prove he wasn't. 'OK, Mr Oldfield. That'll be all for now.'

They went back to the car. Rafferty banged his fist on the

steering wheel. 'If only there was another CCTV camera close to the Staveleys' house. As it is, we've still got nothing – less than nothing.'

'I wouldn't say that. We know Mr Oldfield is a liar. We also have several other strong suspects with no alibis; we've a teenage boy who's run away; we've a husband of the dead woman who had a bad marriage; we've got boyfriends who can't prove their whereabouts at the relevant time. I think we've got a lot. We just require a lucky break, that's all.'

'That's all! Well, I wish this lucky break would hurry up because we need it and we need it now. I thought we had something positive when you found Oldfield's car on the CCTV. It's a big disappointment that it's come to nothing.' Superintendent Bradley didn't like disappointments and tended to give a hard time to those of his officers who brought them to his door.

Disgruntled at their lack of progress, Rafferty drove back to the station, had Llewellyn type up his report of their interview with Gary Oldfield, organized an officer to check out the Chinese takeaway Oldfield said he had gone to – they might remember him if he was a regular customer – and then went home.

Abra was back from work. She gave him a hello kiss, then she questioned him closely as to how the investigation was going as, with the wedding getting ever closer, she was becoming increasingly anxious about the ceremony and whether they would have to cancel.

'How did you get on today?' she asked. 'Are you any closer to catching the killer?'

Was she asking if he was close to finding out her possible involvement in the murder? he wondered. Certainly, there was an edge of concern in her voice. But that could be due to her worry about cancelling the wedding and honeymoon.

Not yet ready to broach the worrying situation that confronted him and which seemed likely to blow up in his face when he did, he strove to keep his voice and manner pleasant and as normal as he could manage. 'I wouldn't say that exactly, sweetheart. But we're working on several leads. Several very promising leads.'

Abra swept her long, chestnut plait over her shoulder. 'So you're saying you're not getting anywhere?'

Was that relief he heard in her voice? 'I wouldn't exactly say that, either.'

'Then what are you saying? Come on, Joe. This is important.'

'I know that. I'm doing my best.' Her badgering almost made him confront her after all. But he managed to bite back the words. 'Something will turn up, you'll see. As I said, I've several promising leads.' He didn't add that he had no evidence for any of them.

'I hope so. I really hope so, as I'm becoming a nervous wreck with the uncertainty of it all.'

So was Rafferty. But he tried to buck up Abra by making more confident noises. He didn't noticeably succeed in mollifying her and after dinner, she went to bed early, saying she had a headache, leaving Rafferty to sit and brood. Was her 'headache' a sign of guilt? Or was it, as she said, only because she was concerned about the wedding? But these were unprofitable thoughts and he soon turned to contemplating the investigation and its progress. Or lack of it as Bradley had said.

Where was he going wrong? he wondered. There must be something else he could do in the investigation. If only Kyle Staveley would turn up, it would give them another line of investigation after the one on Gary Oldfield had come to nothing – the Chinese takeaway had confirmed that Oldfield had come in for a takeaway late on the afternoon of the murder. He had to accept that Llewellyn was right and there would be no time for him to go to the Staveleys' house as well. But his thoughts and hopes were unprofitable and eventually he took himself to bed. Abra was already asleep. He was relieved as it meant he didn't have to pretend that everything was normal between them. Keeping his distance from her prone body, he turned to face the wall.

Their lucky break turned up the next day when Kyle Staveley was traced in London. Rafferty sent one of his officers to town to fetch him back to Elmhurst. On his arrival, he was put in an interview room to wait while Rafferty telephoned his father.

John Staveley must have broken the speed limit he took such a short time to reach the police station. Rafferty went down and met him in reception. 'This way, Mr Staveley.'

Rafferty led him to interview room one and settled him down in a chair next to his son. Llewellyn was hard on their heels and sat down next to Rafferty. He started the tapes running and intoned the details of those present.

'Right, Kyle,' Rafferty began. 'Perhaps you can start by telling us why you ran away.'

There was silence for a full ten seconds before Kyle answered, then he blurted out, 'I was scared.'

'Scared? Scared of what?'

'Scared that you'd think I did it. That I killed Adrienne.'

'And did you?'

'No! No! I wasn't even in the house when she died.'

'We've only your word for that, Kyle.'

'I know I can't prove I didn't kill her, but I'm telling you I didn't do it.' He brushed his black hair out of his eyes. They were damp and he looked as if he were about to cry. Of course, he was sixteen, Rafferty reminded himself. Only a boy and a nervous, uncertain boy at that.

'Where did you go in London? Where did you stay?'

'I found a bed and breakfast place near Liverpool Street Station. I took some money out of my savings account to pay for it. Once I booked in, I stayed in my room, so there was no danger of me being found.'

'But you left the room which is when one of the Metropolitan Police spotted you.'

'Yes. I was hungry. I wanted a McDonald's. The B and B only did breakfast.'

Kyle hadn't planned his escape very well. You'd have thought that, at the least, he'd have bought himself a loaf of bread and a hunk of cheese in preparation for his hermit's existence. His lack of preparation had led to his capture, so they should be grateful. He'd been hauled back to Elmhurst with barely enough time to pack his belongings into his bag. His Great Escape hadn't lasted very long at all.

Was he just a frightened kid? Or was he a murderer, haunted by guilt and desperately trying to protect himself?

Rafferty didn't know, but with no evidence against Kyle he had no choice but to release him into the care of his father. He walked down the stairs with them and saw them off the premises. He watched as Kyle and John Staveley crossed the road, wondering if he'd just let a murderer go free.

After they'd released Kyle, Rafferty went back upstairs to the office. He sent Llewellyn to get tea from the canteen. It helped him think and he drank copious quantities of it every day.

'So much for that,' he said, disgruntled, when Llewellyn returned. 'When the Met rang to say they'd found the boy, I admit I felt hopeful. No longer. We're no further forward than we ever were.'

'Well, at least the boy's been found,' said Llewellyn in an attempt to console him as he put the tea on the desk.

Rafferty snorted. 'Much good it's done us.'

But with no evidence against Kyle – or anyone else for that matter – they had to move on. Superintendent Bradley would insist on it.

Rafferty decided to review what they had so far, so he and Llewellyn divided the statements into two piles and got started. Silence reigned for half an hour. Rafferty finished his now cold tea, then chewed on his fingernails.

'What I don't understand,' he said finally, 'is how all this paperwork amounts to a big pile of nothing. As I said before, we must be going wrong somewhere. Hours of work, of interviews, come to precious little.'

'In that, it's no different from any other case we've dealt with,' said Llewellyn, the voice of reason, as he looked up from his desk. 'We'll get there; we always have before.'

'Mmm, maybe. But this case seems to be shaping up differently. I swear we're longer, this time, getting results.' And if Abra was involved in this death he wasn't sure he wanted a resolution.

'We'll get them. Don't worry. Something will turn up.'

'Well, it's taking its own sweet time. I wish it would hurry up. My wedding's getting nearer by the day. And with each day that passes, Abra's becoming more of a nervous wreck, wondering if we're going to have to cancel. I told her we can still get married, that it's just a case of taking a few hours off, but she's not convinced. And then there's the honeymoon. She's been so looking forward to it and it's not as if my cousin will give me a refund if we have to cancel that as well.'

'Ah. Yes. That's a bit of a knotty problem. Perhaps it wasn't wise booking your honeymoon through your cousin Nigel.'

'Tell me about it. It's too late now. We'll just have to hope for the best, I suppose. There's nothing else we can do. Maybe, if this case doesn't start moving soon, I should go to see Nigel and see if I can't impinge on his better nature.'

'Has he got one?' Llewellyn, who, by now, knew Nigel pretty well, sounded doubtful.

It was unlike the Welshman to propound the negative aspects of the situation. Rafferty was surprised. 'Probably not,' he said. 'But anything's worth a try, if only to make Abra see I'm doing something on the honeymoon front.'

'I suppose so. How is she by the way? Not getting cold feet, I hope?'

'Not so far. Though if this limbo situation continues, I won't rule it out. I can't make her see that it's just as bad for me. Worse, in fact, as everything depends on my bringing the case to a satisfactory conclusion. It all rests on that.'

'Well, at least now you know that Abra had no involvement, don't you?'

Rafferty gave a sickly grin.

'I take it that means you have yet to speak to her about it.'

Rafferty nodded miserably. 'How can I tackle her? You know how she flares up when she thinks she's accused of something. What am I supposed to say – was it John Staveley or his wife that you were having the affair with? Or rather than having an affair with Adrienne, did you kill her and if so, why?'

It was clear that Llewellyn had been thinking along similar lines because he gave a slow nod and said nothing more.

Wishing to change the subject, Rafferty said, 'You know, I think I'll go and see Nigel after work this evening. See if I can't make him show a bit of family solidarity.' Not that that had ever been his cousin's strong point. Nigel tended to shy away from family entanglements more often than not. He thought family overrated and more trouble than it was worth. Sometimes, given the Rafferty clan's love of off-the-back-of-a-lorry bargains, and all the angst it caused him as the family's only copper, Rafferty was inclined to agree with him.

Especially when one or more of the Rafferty clan was getting inveigled into stuff on the wrong side of the law, which wasn't an unusual occurrence. Rafferty sighed and went back to studying statements for a few minutes before he sat back, checked in his pocket for change, and said, 'It's my turn to get tea. Do you fancy a sticky bun?'

Llewellyn shook his head.

But the break from the office and its infernal paperwork didn't last long. He was soon back. Reluctantly, he returned to studying the statements.

It was an unproductive afternoon, and, for all their painstaking perusal of the paperwork, it threw nothing new up. It was after seven when he admitted defeat, told Llewellyn to go home and headed for Nigel's estate agency. It was his cousin's late night, so he knew Nigel should be there.

He was. And not inclined to listen to Rafferty's pleas about refunds.

'No can do, coz. I told you before.'

'I know you did. But have a heart, Nigel. This is our honeymoon I'm talking about. Have you no family feeling?'

'Not so's you'd notice, no. I can't operate one policy for family and another for my other clients. It wouldn't be ethical.'

Rafferty just stopped himself from snorting in disbelief. Ethics wasn't something that Nigel had ever had much truck with. He wondered why his cousin was coming over all moral now. Then his antenna turned to suspicion mode.

'There's no problem with the honeymoon booking, is there? You have paid the money I gave you to the villa owners?'

Nigel gave what, to Rafferty, looked like a guilty grin. 'Of course I have. What else would I do with it?'

'Spend it. Use it to pay your staff.'

When Nigel didn't reply immediately, Rafferty's antenna turned to overdrive. 'You have, haven't you? Used my money to meet a shortfall in the staff wages?'

'No, of course I haven't. What makes you say such a thing?'

'Simply knowing you is enough. Show me the stub of the cheque you've written to pay the villa owners and I might believe you.'

But Nigel couldn't or wouldn't, which Rafferty felt only confirmed his suspicions. And eventually, he wore Nigel down enough to confirm that Rafferty's money had gone nowhere near the owners.

'So what happens to my honeymoon?' he demanded.

'Much the same as would happen to it if you cancelled. Nothing. You don't go.'

'What?'

'Well you seem convinced you're going to have to cancel, so I can't see the difference.'

'I can. I can see a lot of difference. You're a crook, Nigel. A dirty rotten crook. You'd better find the money to sort out my honeymoon or I'll set Abra on you – not to mention the law.'

'Keep your hair on, Joe. I'll sort you something out.'

'Yes, you will. And the something had better be the equivalent of the honeymoon I've booked and paid for.'

'It will be, don't worry. Things are looking up as I've sold several properties recently and am due to get my cut on one of them tomorrow.'

'Good for you. So let's talk about what we're going to book for the honeymoon.'

'Yes, by all means. Let me just get our brochure. Are you still thinking of the south of France?'

'Yes. I want the nearest thing to the villa I booked. Come to that, is there any reason why I can't still have that one?'

'There is, as a matter of fact. The owners have taken it off the books.'

That was something; at least Abra wouldn't be able to blame him for that. 'Give me the brochure,' he said. 'There was one other villa Abra liked the look of when I booked. Perhaps that one's available for the weeks I want.'

Nigel handed over the brochure and Rafferty quickly thumbed his way through till he found the villa that interested him. 'That's the one,' he said. 'Book that one.' He handed the brochure back to Nigel and pointed to the holiday home that interested him.

'Right you are. Consider it done.'

'I won't consider it done till we're ensconced after the wedding and no one comes to ask what we're doing there.'

'They won't. This booking will be firm. I told you – I've now got some money coming in from property sales.'

'Just as long as you don't use my money again to fund another salary shortfall.'

'Fear not. It won't happen.'

'It already has. Just don't do it again or I'll come down on you with all the force of the law.'

'You won't do that.' Nigel sounded confident of his ground.

'You won't want my name joined with yours at the cop shop. You know how hot they are on what they'd probably call undesirables having a family connection with a police officer.'

Rafferty did and his threat was an empty one – just as Nigel had been quick to realize. He said no more about the forces of the law. It was a pointless threat, as the last thing Rafferty wanted was for the station brass to find out his family wasn't whiter than white. His family's tendency to a less than wholehearted honesty had bedevilled his career. It was only sheer luck that this propensity hadn't got back to the brass. And he didn't know how long such luck could last. It had already had a good innings.

They fixed up the alternative honeymoon and Rafferty drove home.

Abra was still on tenterhooks about their wedding arrangements. She'd been a bag of nerves recently. Rafferty could only hope that it was just the wedding that was concerning her.

'Any news on the murder investigation?' she asked eagerly the minute Rafferty stepped through the door of the flat.

'Things are progressing,' was all that Rafferty said.

'Yes, but *how* are they progressing?' Abra wasn't to be put off. 'For good or ill?'

'For good, of course. Kyle Staveley's been found and is back home.'

'So was he the killer?'

'I don't think so. I don't know. But at least he's back and can be questioned again.'

'And that's it? The sole product of the day?'

'Give us a chance, Abra. It's only been a few weeks. You're worse than the superintendent.'

'No one could be worse than him,' Abra replied. 'Certainly not me. Tell me, though, Joe, are you really no further forward?'

Rafferty sighed and knew he'd have to come clean. 'Not so's you'd notice,' he said. 'We've several possibilities, strong possibilities. We just need to wait for the evidence to catch up with them.'

'Is that all?' Abra flounced off to the kitchen and began to dish up their meal. Rafferty followed her.

'It's not that bad,' Rafferty told her as he put the kettle on and brought mugs out of the cupboard. 'It's more a matter of time than anything else.'

'Yes. Time we haven't got. It's less than a week to the wedding now and everything's still up in the air.'

'It won't be. I promise.'

'How can you make such a promise?' Abra demanded as she turned round and waved a potato-smeared wooden spoon at him. She turned back and began to spoon mash on to the plates with the faggots and peas.

Rafferty didn't answer. He concentrated on making the tea instead. He felt it was safer. For both of them.

TEN

Rafferty was late up the next morning. He'd tossed and turned for most of the night thinking about the wedding and honeymoon and how he was to sort out both issues. Not to mention his other worry, the one about Abra's behaviour. The facts said she was either a suspected criminal or as near to an adulteress as it was possible to be without being married.

It had been dawn before he finally slept, still with the various problems unresolved. He just hoped he didn't have to cancel *this* honeymoon and that Nigel hadn't pocketed the payment again. But even Nigel wouldn't do the dirty on him twice. Rather, he didn't think he would, but who could tell with his wily cousin? Nigel did as much ducking and diving as Del Boy Trotter and was generally able to talk himself out of whatever hole he landed in.

He did without a shower to save time and considered not shaving, but the ribald comments he could expect at the station if he did so made him think again. Even so, the shave was a perfunctory one and with not so much as a cup of tea to sustain him, he left for the station.

Llewellyn, of course, was there before him, looking as bright-eyed and bushy tailed as a squirrel. The sight of his sergeant made him groan inwardly. He could do without a raring to go Llewellyn. He hoped the start of his day wasn't a pointer to how the rest of it would go.

'Anything new come in?' Rafferty asked as he sat down behind his desk.

Llewellyn shook his head as he turned round. 'Nothing of interest. Do you want some fresh tea? The one I got earlier must be lukewarm by now.'

Llewellyn's subtle way of saying he was late didn't escape Rafferty. He sipped his tea experimentally. 'No. This one's all right.' He downed it in one before it got cooler. 'I suppose we'd better go and see our main suspects again,' he said. 'Badger them a bit and see what comes out.'

'Don't you think we should go and see Abra and question her about why her fingerprints were found all over the Staveleys' home?'

'What – beard her in her place of work? She'd love that. No. Leave Abra to me. I'll speak to her.'

'When?'

'Soon.' He'd have to. He had no choice really. His greatest horror was that he might have to charge her with murder. The thought of this was infinitely worse than the possibility of infidelity and that was bad enough.

'OK. You know your own business best. So who do you want to see first?'

'Gary Oldfield springs to mind. He's still looking tasty to my way of thinking. He could still have done it. He could have rung through to the Chinese takeaway and ordered his meal and driven straight to the Staveleys' house.'

'He looks no more interesting than anyone else, surely?'

'Yes he does. He lied to us, remember and induced his girl-friend to lie to us as well. Why lie if he's not got something to hide?'

'Maybe because he didn't want us to know that he had been out and about near the Staveleys' home at the relevant time.'

'Why should he be worried? Unless he knew he had reason to kill Adrienne. What if he didn't tell Adrienne about his live-in girlfriend and she found out about her? Could provide a reason for violence, with his retaliating a touch too far. I always did reckon he had a nasty streak, so I wouldn't put it past him. It wouldn't be premeditated, granted, but I can still see him killing her accidentally. And he was out and about near the Staveleys' home at the right time. I know the Chinese takeaway confirmed that he came in for a meal that evening. It's a shame that they can't remember if he placed his order over the phone or came in and ordered, but, as I said, he might still have gone on to Adrienne's place and killed her.'

'Time's a bit tight, even if he ordered his meal by tele-phone. We've got him on CCTV both going to the Chinese and returning. The time lapse is no more than fifteen minutes.'

'Even so. He might just have managed to squeeze her in.'

Llewellyn looked doubtful. His next words proved he was determined to play Devil's advocate. 'Anyway, why would Mrs Staveley care about the live-in girlfriend? She had a

husband as well as two other men who admit to being her
lovers and whom she mentioned in her diary – she could
hardly object if Oldfield had another woman.'

'You're not taking the unreasonableness of women into
account. What's sauce for the goose isn't necessarily sauce
for the gander. No, it's a fair assumption. Let's go and ask
Oldfield if Adrienne knew about Diana Rexton.'

Gary Oldfield was at work in the used car lot on Station
Road and not very pleased to see them after they parked up
outside the lot and threaded their way through the parked cars
towards him.

'What do you want now?' he demanded. 'I've told you all
I know. What else do you expect from me?' He scowled at
Rafferty and threw a dirty look in Llewellyn's direction.

Rafferty took no notice of the scowl or the dirty look and
said sternly, 'I expect your co-operation, Mr Oldfield. As I
said to you before, this is a murder inquiry. We'll ask as many
questions as many times as necessary to get at the truth. For
instance, I'm interested to learn if Adrienne Staveley knew
about your girlfriend.'

'Of course Adrienne knew. She didn't care. She wasn't
looking for a long-term relationship. It was only ever a bit of
fun.'

'So you say. But her diary says differently. Her diary says
she was pressurizing you to set up home together.'

'Well, she wasn't. Or not much. She knew very well that
it wasn't on. I'd told her several times.'

'Which indicates persistence on her part.' Rafferty smiled.
'But I suppose I'll have to take your word for it that she
wasn't pushing for the togetherness act in some little love
nest, won't I?'

'So you should, 'cos it's true. Now, was there anything else
as I've got work to do.'

There were no customers hovering eager to get ripped off
by Oldfield, so Rafferty didn't know what work could be so
urgent. However, he said, 'No. I think that's it for now. Thank
you for your time.'

'Always happy to help the police.'

'Glad to hear it. Goodbye, Mr Oldfield. No doubt I'll see
you again.'

Oldfield scowled a second time at this, then he turned away

and made for the Portakabin. He stood in the doorway watching them till they drove away.

'Think he was telling the truth about Adrienne being aware of his girlfriend?' Rafferty asked as he did up his seatbelt. 'She makes no mention of it in her diary.'

From Devil's advocate, Llewellyn perversely took the opposite stance. 'I don't know. But he would say that, wouldn't he? There's no one to contradict him.'

'Mmm. Right. Let's go and see the Staveleys again. See if there's any more we can get out of him and his son. I still don't like the fact that Kyle ran away. It strikes me as suspicious. With all those simmering teenage emotions, it would be the work of seconds for him to strangle Adrienne, then after a day or two of agonizing about it, to run away in fright at what he'd done.'

'And what about his father? Do you think he's covering up for Kyle?'

'I don't know. But if John Staveley didn't kill her himself, he must have a few suspicions about his son's guilt, though whether the boy has confessed to his father is another matter.'

The Staveleys were both at home. John Staveley explained that Kyle had a home study period and it seemed that since his wife's death, Staveley himself had abandoned his pounding of the streets, which was revealing in itself of how poor their relationship had been.

Once seated in the living room, Rafferty didn't waste any time. 'We've been looking into your wife's life, Mr Staveley,' he said. 'And it seems she was a woman who liked a good time.'

'Yes. She missed the money when I was made redundant. It meant we couldn't afford to entertain. Or not in the way that we and our friends were used to.'

Not being able to afford to entertain was one thing, but to learn your wife was a promiscuous slapper was something else. That was, if it *was* news to Staveley. But either way, it was news that had to be broken and Rafferty broke it. 'Not only that – she also liked men friends and had several. In fact, we've discovered at least two of them were her lovers. Did you know?'

'Lovers? Adrienne? No, of course I didn't know. How would

I?' He paused then, as if he thought it prudent to ask, and said, 'Who were they?'

'That's not important. What is important is whether one of her lovers had anything to do with her death.'

'And do you think they might have?'

'It's a possibility, nothing more at this stage.'

'She certainly had plenty of time to entertain men friends,' Staveley said bitterly. 'She's not worked since we married and was on her own all day. As you know, I left the house in the morning and stayed out till evening, every day. Kyle did the same.'

What sad, separate lives this family had lived, was Rafferty's thought. At least now, with Adrienne gone, they felt able to spend time in their own home, rather than wander the streets or make use of the local library's facilities.

'You didn't know any of her men friends?' Rafferty now asked.

'No. We pretty much lived separate lives. Anyway, how do you know she had lovers?'

'She kept a diary. A very explicit diary.'

'I see.' His face tightened as he took this in. It looked thinner, as if he had lost weight. In fact, he looked gaunt and more Draculaesque than ever. 'So there's no doubt about these lovers you say she had?'

'No, sir. None at all.'

Staveley nodded at this, but said nothing more on the subject.

Rafferty reflected again on the sadness of their marriage. He hoped he and Abra never came to such a pass. Always supposing they were still together by the time the wedding came round . . .

'You're sure you didn't suspect your wife's extramarital liaisons?' What was it that Llewellyn had said? That the husband was the last to know. He and Abra were already man and wife in all but the paperwork. Was he being played for a cuckold like John Staveley? Was that why Staveley had taken a mistress?

'I didn't know she had lovers.' The answer was sharp. 'I had no idea. I told you. I was hardly ever here, apart from in the evenings. And then I shut myself away in the study. Adrienne did her own thing – she always did, even when I was working, she never changed her plans to accommodate me or my son.'

'I see. Tell me, did your son ever meet any of your wife's men friends?'

'I don't know. Kyle?' Staveley turned questioning eyes on his son.

Kyle reacted like a startled rabbit. He shot forward in his chair and blushed furiously.

'Kyle?' Rafferty encouraged.

After several seconds and with a clear degree of reluctance, he answered in the affirmative. 'Yes. Once. I came home from school one day because I was ill and there was a strange man here. She didn't introduce us. I just went up to my room and stayed there. I heard them come upstairs shortly after and go into her bedroom. They didn't seem to care that I was in the house. I could hear them through the wall. They made no effort to keep quiet.'

John Staveley looked shattered at this revelation. It was one thing for one's wife to have lovers, his expression seemed to say. But quite another to flaunt his humiliation and her infidelity in front of his son.

'You didn't think of confiding in your father?'

With a quick, faintly apologetic glance at Staveley, Kyle said, 'God no. How could I? He was already stressed after being made redundant. To learn his wife was having sex with another man in his own house . . .'

Poor lad. What a discovery to have made. Adrienne Staveley must have been a shameless bitch. Rafferty was really beginning to dislike her. He wasn't surprised that she had been murdered. Her behaviour was such as to invite violence. She must have been an extraordinarily blinkered woman not to see beyond her own immediate pleasures. John Staveley and his son had had a lot to put up with. Had it led one of them to murder?

Rafferty couldn't altogether blame them if it had. But it was still his job to catch Adrienne's killer, no matter how distasteful actually slapping the cuffs on might be.

They left soon after. Rafferty had intended questioning Mrs Staveley Senior again, but when they stopped at her house it was to discover that she wasn't home, so they called a halt to the interviews and went back to the station.

'What a cow Adrienne was,' said Rafferty once they were back in the office. 'Imagine just continuing with her sex jinks with her stepson in the house. What a situation to put the poor boy in. Serve her right if he'd told his father. Fancy carrying on like that in front of an impressionable lad.'

'Yes. It is pretty despicable,' Llewellyn agreed. 'She must have been a very selfish woman.'

'You can say that again. I think I'd have been tempted to murder her myself if she'd been my wife. I wonder why Staveley didn't divorce her.'

'Probably couldn't afford it. From what we've learned of her she was likely to sting him for every penny.'

'Poor sod. What a situation to find yourself in. Wonder why he married her as some of her selfish traits must have been evident before they got hitched. She seems to have been keen on between the sheets sport, so I suppose it was the sex.'

'It usually is,' was Llewellyn's world-weary comment.

'Oh well. Get the interviews typed up and then we'll get some lunch. The Black Swan suit you?'

'Yes. Sounds good.'

The reports on the interviews with Oldfield and the Staveleys didn't take Llewellyn long and they were soon headed out for lunch.

The Black Swan was an attractive pub on the banks of the – at the moment – not-so-Sniffey Tiffey and served excellent meals at lunchtime. Rafferty chose roast lamb with all the trimmings and Llewellyn had salmon and spinach with creamed potatoes.

The staff were efficient and their meals were quickly served. They tucked in with relish. They were quiet for some time as they enjoyed the good food, but when they had finished and were sipping their drinks, they discussed the case some more.

'Oldfield's become favourite with me,' said Rafferty. 'Even though his girlfriend provided him with an alibi, it fell at the first hurdle. Though the more I learn about Adrienne the more I have to say that John Staveley is a close second. I wish we could get some evidence either way. The case is moving way too slowly for my liking.'

'Yes, it does seem sluggish. But I'm convinced something will happen to speed things up.'

'Like what?' Rafferty sipped his Adnam's Bitter morosely.

'I think a witness will eventually come out of the woodwork.'

'I wish they'd hurry up.' As long as this metaphorical witness didn't implicate Abra. 'The case has had enough publicity to bring every witness out of the woodwork.' He paused and put his beer down. 'So who do you think is the killer?'

The habitually cautious Llewellyn wasn't prepared to commit himself and told Rafferty that he was a 'don't know'.

'Can't you plump for someone for once?' Rafferty asked peevishly. 'You're always sitting on the fence.'

'But as you said, we've no firm evidence against any of the suspects, so how can I plump for a particular one? They all had the opportunity and some had a definite motive.'

'That's the trouble. Too many suspects and motives, yet precious few clues. Oh well . . .' Rafferty drained his beer. 'Want another mineral water?'

'No thanks. I think we should be getting back.'

'Before the super starts looking for us, you mean?'

'Just so.'

But fortunately, according to Bill Beard on reception, Bradley hadn't been on the prowl and they got back to their office without meeting him. Rafferty gave a sigh of relief. Bradley was getting ever more tetchy about the investigation and its slow progress. Always keen to impress Region, the super liked his cases to progress smoothly with no hitches or delays, so the situation with this case didn't suit him at all. Just let him find out about Abra . . .

ELEVEN

Superintendent Bradley stayed away from them for the rest of the day, much to Rafferty's relief. He didn't feel up to defending his corner against Bradley's unreasonableness yet again. The man was insupportable and shouldn't be in charge of staff. Once again, Rafferty found himself wishing that Bradley would get promotion to Region and thus be out of his hair. Let him promulgate politically correct dogma for the force to adhere to; that was about his mark.

Reports were still coming in as the questioning of potential witnesses continued, but none of them told them anything new. The most prominent of the potential witnesses that had come forward had long ago been questioned and there remained only the dregs and the attention seekers to be interviewed, which tasks Rafferty mostly left to the team to undertake.

'We've got to start thinking outside the box,' Rafferty told Llewellyn as he threw the negative reports down on his desk in disgust.

Llewellyn twisted round in his chair and fixed his intelligent brown gaze on Rafferty. 'What box would that be?'

'The box that we've managed to shut ourselves up in. The box of the official investigation. We've been too blinkered, done too much thinking in straight lines. It might explain why we haven't got anywhere.'

Llewellyn's thinly handsome face grew longer as he considered this. 'We've been through all the usual procedures and—'

'Exactly. Sticking to the rules. That's what we've been doing. Maybe we ought to start breaking a few rules.'

'Like what?' Llewellyn looked faintly alarmed. The Welshman was a rules and regulations sort of guy and was always wary of Rafferty's more outrageous suggestions.

'Like forgetting about Superintendent Bradley and his desire to impress Region, for a start. He's kept our noses to the grindstone for long enough with no result. Let's just forget about him altogether and do our own thing.'

'Which would be?'

'I don't know, do I?' Rafferty picked up a paperclip and twisted it savagely. 'Just something other than we've been doing. Something, anything that might give us a lead. Maybe setting a watch on our main suspects and hopefully spooking them.' Particularly Gary Oldfield, he thought.

'I can't see Superintendent Bradley authorizing that. Think of the overtime. Think of the budgetary constraints imposed by the latest financial cutbacks.'

Rafferty didn't want to think about them and said so.

'Why don't we try questioning each of the suspects again?' Llewellyn suggested instead.

They had already questioned them all several times, to no avail. Not one of them had betrayed any degree of guilt or desire to confess and without a confession they had nothing meaty on any of them bar their dislike of the dead woman and the circumstantial evidence that they couldn't prove where they were between four and six o'clock on the day she was murdered.

Rafferty didn't see any point in doing this. 'No. Not just now. That can wait. Not that we've got anything from any of them – apart from learning that none of them has an alibi worthy of the name.'

'All the more reason to investigate them further, I would have thought. A lack of an alibi on a suspect's part surely indicates the need for further questioning.'

'Yes. And we will. Just not yet. I want to approach the case from another angle.'

'Which would be?' Llewellyn asked again.

The Welshman had an unfortunate habit of going into interrogation mode when Rafferty started to put ideas forward. He supposed it was down to his university education and his membership of the debating society. Whatever brought it on, it got on Rafferty's nerves and he answered sharply. 'As I said – I don't know – yet. I'm working on it. Something will occur to me.' Rafferty just hoped the something occurred to him soon, or he wouldn't be able to deflect Bradley's desire to look good at Region and his liability to come down hard on officers who failed to supply the goods to enable him to do so.

'Tell me, Dafyd – what have we done so far on the case?'

Let him answer a few question for a change, instead of interrogating *him*.

'As I said, we've done all the usual things. Questioned everyone with a connection to the victim. All as normal.'

'All as normal. And where has it got us? Nowhere. We have to approach this from a new angle. Any ideas?'

'No.'

'Nor have I. It's a bugger, isn't it?'

The frustrating day finally ended and Rafferty went home to Abra. He stopped to pick up an Indian takeaway on the way after ringing home to check that she hadn't made a start on dinner: he liked to get takeaways several times a week to save Abra from cooking. She worked all day, as did he, but she invariably got home before him so she generally started preparing the evening meal.

Abra was glad to see him. 'And you've brought our dinner, too. Well done, that man. Brownie points for you.'

'Tell God and he can put it on the plus side of his Great Book,' Rafferty told her as he led the way into the kitchen. 'Any news on your flat sale?'

'Yes. I had an offer on it today,' Abra told him as he began to dish up.

Abra had her own flat, on St Mark's Road, which she'd bought before she'd met him. It was the place she had retreated to when she had left him over their different views on the wedding costs. He'd be glad when it was sold, then if she decided to leave him again at least she wouldn't have a ready bolthole to go to. Unless, that was, she was having an affair with John Staveley. In which case she'd have a large and comfortable house to retreat to, a house, moreover, that was bigger than anything he could afford to buy her.

Once again, he recalled Sam Dally's remarks as to Abra being young enough and attractive enough to find a partner who didn't work long hours, many of which were often unpaid, who earned more and who didn't break family arrangements at a moment's notice. What Sam had said had preyed on his mind ever since, especially given Abra's fingerprints in Staveley's bedroom. He really must find the courage to ask her about it without antagonizing her. She was liable to fly off the handle if she thought he was accusing her of something – and what could he be accusing her of but having an affair? Unless she had killed Adrienne Staveley. Though that wouldn't explain her fingerprints all over the house, more particularly, they wouldn't explain their presence in Staveley's monkish bedroom.

He forced such unwelcome reflections from his mind and said, 'Really? That's great. Is it a good offer?'

'I think so.' She mentioned a figure and Rafferty nodded.

'Who was it? A young couple?'

'No, a young guy. He seemed very keen, according to the estate agent. Well, he must have been to make an offer. Now perhaps we could do likewise on the house I fell in love with.'

Abra had set her heart on a semi-detached house they had viewed. It was on the outskirts of Elmhurst, but not on an estate. It was an older, character property with three spacious bedrooms and an open fireplace in each of the two reception rooms. There was even a small conservatory and a green-house, which had really pleased Abra, as she had green fingers and liked to grow things. She'd been very restricted in the flat with just a windowsill for herbs.

'Yes. That'll be great. I'll ring the agents tomorrow.' Rafferty picked up the plates and made for the living room. 'Bring the cutlery,' he shouted over his shoulder.

Soon, they were tucking into Abra's favourite: Chicken Tikka Masala and making swift inroads into the food: surprisingly, for Abra, who was quite adventurous in other ways, her taste in Indian food was typically British and lacking in experiment. Why try something new? she said, when I may not like it and I'll go hungry.

Rafferty got up. 'Fancy a drink, sweetheart?'

'Yes please.'

Rafferty poured two glasses of Jameson's, brought them to the table and sat down again. Their drinks bill at the local supermarket was becoming excessive, as they got through four bottles of Jameson's whiskey a week as well as wine and beer. Rafferty's ma told him he drank too much and he supposed she was right, but it had become a habit that – in the way of such things – he'd settled into. 'So what's happening on the case?' Abra asked before she bit into a poppadom. She'd asked the same question every night since the investigation had begun, such was her anxiety about cancelling the wedding. Unfortunately, the answer was the same as it had been on each of the previous occasions.

'Not a lot' was Rafferty's reluctant admission. He spooned the last of the rice and chicken into his mouth, chewed and swallowed, hoping the pause would give him time to think of something hopeful to tell her. But nothing occurred to him.

'There must be something else you can do. What about your snouts? Haven't they been any help?'

'No. Most of the suspects are pretty respectable citizens, so wouldn't come into the orbit of snouts.'

'What about that other feller – the used car salesman. He must be a bit dodgy. Surely one of your snouts can find out something useful on him if they put the word out.'

'I've already tried. There's been nothing.'

'Well, try again. Things change. It could be worthwhile.' When she saw he didn't look too enthusiastic at her suggestion, she said, 'Go on, love. Try again. Promise me?'

'OK. I promise.' Though he didn't hold out much hope that anything useful would come of it.

'Good. So what are we to do about the wedding? Should I ring Father Kelly and cancel?'

'No.' He sounded more vehement than he had intended. But for her to cancel the wedding was the last thing he wanted her to do. To him it would indicate that any affair with Staveley was a serious one and she was using his lack of success at finding Adrienne Staveley's killer as a smokescreen to post-pone their wedding. He hoped he wasn't tempting the fates when he said, 'We'll get married whatever happens, though the honeymoon might have to go on the back burner for a short while.'

'Great. So what's the position on the insurance?'

There was no position on the insurance. They didn't have any insurance. Rafferty, having so much on his mind, had again forgotten to arrange any, though, knowing Nigel, he'd only pocket the money if he had organized cover. 'All in hand,' Rafferty temporized. 'We'll get our honeymoon, never fear.'

'I hope so.'

'It'll happen, Abra. Believe me. It might be delayed by a few weeks, but we'll still be going to France.' France was a new destination for them. Usually they holidayed in Spain or

Greece or the Canary Islands, but Abra had recently decided to take an evening class in French conversation to help her converse with foreign agents in the theatrical agency in which she worked. They had plumped for the south of France, so they could get sun *and* conversation.

'Good. Get me another drink, will you, Joe?'

'Coming right up.' Rafferty poured the Jameson's and handed Abra her glass. 'Here's to us,' he said as he chinked glasses. He crossed his fingers under the table as he added, 'And to our future together.' He hoped he wasn't tempting fate and that they *did* have a future together.

'To us,' Abra echoed. 'But Joe, what do you think are the chances that we'll still be able to go on honeymoon for the two weeks we booked?'

'Fair to middling,' he told her as he kept his fingers crossed. 'Stop fretting, sweetheart. It'll happen. Believe me.'

'I hope you're right. I'm not optimistic.'

'Be optimistic, Abracadabra. I'm working on it.'

'I know you are, Joe. Just try a bit harder.'

'I will. I'm doing my best, sweetpea.'

'Yes. I know you are,' Abra said again. 'Just keep trying hard, my love and we won't have to cancel anything.'

'I will,' Rafferty echoed in turn. Her words renewed his hope that she wasn't having an affair and that he'd find, if – no, when – he asked her about the presence of her fingerprints all over the Staveleys' house, that she'd be able to supply a rational explanation. It seemed unlikely. However, he strove for optimism. 'You'll see. It'll come right before the honeymoon.'

'Let's drink to it.'

They chinked glasses again. 'To our wedding and honeymoon,' said Rafferty.

'To our wedding and honeymoon,' Abra repeated.

They went to bed soon after and, once again, Rafferty tossed and turned, unable to sleep, as his worry gene went into overdrive. His mind turned to the honeymoon again. Always supposing it happened. He didn't want to disappoint Abra – he'd disappointed her enough in the past. Perhaps that was why . . . but no, he wasn't going to go there. Still, unless he could hit on the solution to the case her disappointment was likely to be inevitable. And he didn't want that. She'd had occasion already in their relationship to discover that he had feet of clay and the last thing he wanted was for her to make the same discovery again.

If she really was thinking of leaving him, then giving her yet another reason, on top of the job, for her to go, wasn't a good idea.

TWELVE

Surprisingly, the new day brought with it a new optimism. Even the sun was shining as if to cast its approval on such unreasonable hopefulness. Rafferty sprang out of bed, showered and took Abra her tea, then set off for work with a sprightly gait. He didn't know where these new rosy expectations had come from or why they had appeared, but he was grateful for it. It beat the downbeat mood of previous days. Maybe it would even give him the courage to ask Abra about her relationship with the Staveley family.

'What ho, Dafyd,' he said as he entered the office. 'What's new?'

Even Llewellyn's reply of 'not much', didn't dampen his enthusiasm for the day ahead.

'Never mind. I've had a new lease of life. We're going to get somewhere today, I feel it in my bones.'

'Really? That's good. You've given up your thoughts of out-of-the-box rule-breaking?' Llewellyn's voice took on an upward lilt, as if pleased at this.

Rafferty killed the hope. 'Not at all. I'm still deciding which of the many rules that constrict us, to break. I'll let you know when I come up with one. No, I woke this morning feeling all's well with the world and I'm sure the day won't disappoint me.'

In spite of Rafferty's newfound optimism, it was clear that Llewellyn didn't share it. 'I hope you're right,' he said with a downward turn to his voice.

So do I, thought Rafferty as a little of the previous pessimism returned to haunt him. But his optimism wasn't to be dented, not even by Llewellyn's lacklustre response.

'So, update me on the latest reports,' he said. 'Anything of any interest?'

'No.'

'Tell me the worst – don't hold back whatever you do.'

'There is no worst, as such, just nothing good or helpful.'

'Same old, same old, then. Oh well. Time for tea.' He took

a large gulp of the tea Llewellyn got from the canteen each morning. It helped him think. In fact his first few sips gave him a brainwave. Why didn't he ask *John Staveley* what Abra's fingerprints were doing in his bedroom? He might surprise the man into an admission, though of course, there was the danger that he'd let the cat out of the bag to others, which Rafferty didn't want. Still, it was something worth thinking about, especially if he received a reassuring answer concerning Abra's presence in the house. Though, for the life of him, he couldn't imagine what such a reassuring answer might consist of.

They sipped as they looked through the latest reports. But Llewellyn was right. There was nothing of interest in any of them. Even the roadside survey team near the Staveleys' home hadn't produced anything new. Rafferty finished the rest of his tea and sat back. 'Now what?' he asked, not really expecting an answer, but feeling obliged to ask the question in the hope that Llewellyn would inspire him.

'I don't know,' said Llewellyn. 'I'm plumb out of ideas.'

'And me. But we'd better come up with something soon or Bradley'll go ballistic. You know what he's like.'

'Mmm. There is one thing – Gary Oldfield's girlfriend has form.'

'What, Diana Rexton? You do surprise me. She struck me as the honest type. So what did she do? Rob some of the pick and mix from Woolies when she was ten, as a dare?'

'No. And you're right – she is honest. At least as far as Woolworth and other stores are concerned. But not as regards Mr Oldfield, of course. You haven't forgotten that she must have lied about him being with her when Mrs Staveley was murdered?'

'No. I haven't forgotten. In fact, she's on my list to be questioned about it. Anyway, so what did she do?'

'Assault. It seems that, like her horse, she has a temper. She attacked a woman she thought was flirting with Mr Oldfield.'

'Did she now? That's interesting. Is that it? The only thing against her?'

'That's it.'

'Still, it's something. Shows a propensity for violence in the name of love, if nothing else. She didn't go for this woman's throat by any chance?'

'No. She punched her. Knocked her out, apparently.'

'Pity. And there was me thinking she's such a nice lady.'

'Not so much the lady to have done such a thing,' said the Methodist-raised Llewellyn primly.

'Too right. So we've established that she's got a violent streak. She's the only suspect we've got who's shown such a predilection. Pity her car doesn't show up on the CCTV.'

'Isn't it? There again, is Gary Oldfield the man to incite murder?'

'Wouldn't have thought so. But who knows with women? They're an unpredictable sex at the best of times. And she seems potty about him.'

'Mmm. But we've no other evidence against her.'

'We now know Oldfield wasn't at home from five o'clock till around quarter past five, so she's no one to corroborate that *she* was at home during that time. Not that I'd believe Oldfield if he said she was and was up to her neck in asses' milk.'

'Doesn't make her guilty.'

'I didn't say it did.' Rafferty wouldn't give it up easily. 'Still, she's moved up from innocent girlfriend, to wronged potential spouse with a violent streak.'

'I can't see one woman strangling another. Strangling isn't a woman's crime.'

'No. I know. You've already said. So what now?'

'More questioning of the suspects, I presume.'

'Yes. One of them did it. It's just a matter of finding the guilty party. Piece of cake.'

'If you say so.'

'I just did, didn't I? Must be true. There's a limited cast of suspects, none with an alibi. Couldn't be simpler.'

'Ah, but it could be, couldn't it?'

'There's the rub. Yes it could be. I don't know where we're going with this case, Dafyd, and that's flat. What we need is a miracle.'

'I don't think we need a miracle, as such. More a piece or two of good luck.'

'Whatever. There's no sign of either of these desirable items. So it's back to the drawing board with everyone involved in the case. I want every suspect's story checked again. I know that none of them has an alibi, but they might be hiding something else relevant to the case – though God knows what it could be, as I don't.'

He went out just before lunch in an attempt to fulfil the promise he'd made to Abra about contacting his snouts. Nowadays, police officers weren't supposed to have exclusive handling rights on snouts, but were meant to share them with at least one other officer. Rafferty tended to bend this rule. He'd done the work of cultivation, so he didn't see why he should share his snouts with any other officers, particularly if it meant their arrest record turned out better than his own. Why provide Superintendent Bradley with ammunition to use against him?

He did the rounds of the local pubs and managed to find two of his snouts that he hadn't seen in a while.

Jimmy Mack was an old-time criminal with more jail time than Nelson Mandela. Like Rafferty, he didn't believe in informant registration: he didn't like being monitored by authority. He'd had enough of that after spending so many years in jail, so he was more than happy to accommodate Rafferty's desire for an exclusive arrangement.

Rafferty's other informant hadn't been able to help him, but Jimmy Mack seemed to have something useful. At least that was what he implied. He bought the old man a large Scotch and started to pump him. 'What can you tell me about McGann's Used Cars?' he asked. 'I'm particularly interested in their salesman, Gary Oldfield.'

'Oldfield. I know him. Sold a car to a friend of mine. It was never any good. It spent most of its time in the garage. He went back to the lot demanding they honour their paltry three-month warranty, but they didn't want to know. Made out it was something he'd done that caused the problem.'

Rafferty frowned and took a large gulp of his Adnam's Bitter. He wasn't interested in tales of old bangers going wrong. That was what old bangers did. 'Can't you tell me anything else more useful to me. It is a murder case I'm investigating.'

'It's a terrible violent world we live in, Mr Rafferty.' Jimmy Mack shook his head and managed to drain his glass at the same time. He slapped his lips and said, 'More of the same would go down a treat. These chilly British summers get into me bones.'

Rafferty sighed and took the hint. When he came back it

was to find Jimmy had ordered a beef sandwich and told the girl to put it on Rafferty's tab.

'I knew you wouldn't mind, Mr Rafferty. Me old bones need some decent protein.'

'I think your old bones are doing pretty well today.' Rafferty put the second Scotch on the table and sat down. He took his wallet out and, under the table, he extracted a twenty-pound note. He screwed it up and shoved it into Jimmy's gnarled right hand.

'Thank you, sir.'

'I want more than thanks. I want something helpful. I've bought you some decent protein and part of your required daily liquid intake, now sell me some decent information.'

'I heard tell that this Oldfield is involved in selling ringers – and cut and shunts – cars that have been involved in accidents and welded together with another car to make one complete vehicle.'

'I know what cut and shunt means. What's that to do with my murder?'

'Nothing, I suppose. I just thought you'd like to know.'

'So now I know. What else have you got?'

'He's a bit of a boyo where the ladies are concerned. I've seen him in here with several different women, yet I heard tell he's meant to be living with some bint.'

'Again – what's that to do with my murder?'

'I'm just giving you a bit of character background, aren't I? No need to be snippy.'

Rafferty did his best to keep his impatience in check. He went up to the bar and bought a third large one, in the hope that the extra liquor would loosen Jimmy's tongue.

It did the trick. Because as he cradled the glass, Jimmy became far more voluble.

'Don't quote me, but I heard on the grapevine that he siphons petrol out of the cars for sale and uses it in his own car. He's been heard to boast that he never has to buy petrol. And that his own car stays in good nick because more often than not he borrows one of the for sale vehicles when he has to go on a longish trip. The old man who owns the firm seems to let him do what he likes. He's lost interest in the business. In poor health, or so I understand.'

'This is all very fascinating, Jimmy, but it's not much use

to me. Have you got any info that's tied in with this murder or not?'

Jimmy downed his last Scotch quickly as if he feared it might be snatched away from him and sat back with a sulky expression. 'I reckon I've given you plenty for a measly twenty. There's fraud, surely and theft. And taking without consent. Not a bad haul.'

'Don't sulk. You're too old to get away with it.'

Jimmy Mack pulled a sarcastic smile. It displayed his teeth. Rafferty had expected the decayed old brown jobs that the ex-con had sported last time he'd seen him, but these were large and sparkling white. He must have got some dental treatment during his latest spell in the nick. The teeth looked incongruous in Jimmy's seamed, cigarette-tanned face. 'OK,' he said. 'It's a fair cop. I've had my fun. Oldfield's a slimy type with a nasty temper on him. The firm's got a young lad that comes in to valet the cars, polish them up and so on.'

'Yes. I know what valeting entails. I wish you'd get on with it and stop telling me what I already know.'

'Word is they had an argument and Oldfield beat him up. Pretty badly, or so I heard. You lot were involved, but nothing came of it. The kid ended up in hospital.'

It was the first Rafferty had heard of it. 'Go on.'

'That's it. Isn't it enough? I've given you three pieces of information and thrown in a fourth as a bonus. You've only given me a measly twenty quid. I reckon you owe me a tenner.'

Their new investigation into the suspects' stories revealed some interesting anomalies. Gary Oldfield had admitted that he'd gone out once to collect a takeaway. So why did his car show up on CCTV late on the evening of the murder? Why would he need to lie about it when it could have no bearing on Adrienne Staveley's death? Where had he been going and to what purpose? And why – once again – had Diana Rexton not mentioned it? Of course, it had been late. Eleven o'clock. And she might have been in bed and asleep. But her seeming complicity in the cover up of what Rafferty regarded as Oldfield's guilt left a sour taste. So much for his nose for the truth. He was getting older, he reminded himself. Perhaps this trait that had served him so well during his long career was starting to fade. He hoped not as it was the only advantage he had against the university-educated Llewellyn.

And then there was his girlfriend. She had lied about Oldfield being at home at the relevant time. Was she scared he had killed Adrienne? Did she have reason to think so? Then again, she had good reason to suspect he was having an affair even though she hadn't found the courage to challenge him about it.

'Give them a bell, Dafyd,' said Rafferty. 'Let's have them both in. See what they have to say for themselves.'

Gary Oldfield and his girlfriend came in after the working day was over. Oldfield was indignant at being questioned again and called into the police station, and made his feelings plain in no uncertain terms.

They decided to interview Oldfield first and leave Diana Rexton to cool her heels in reception. She didn't seem in any rush to undergo an interrogation; in fact, she looked scared out of her wits and tended to cling to Oldfield, who only just managed to curb his impatience at this.

Oldfield was shown to one of the interview rooms.

Once Rafferty had collected Llewellyn, they sat down in the interview room and after he had set the tapes recording, he said, 'So, Mr Oldfield, perhaps you can tell me why you failed to mention that you went out later on the night of Mrs Staveley's murder?'

'Mention it? Why would I mention it?' Oldfield leaned back in his chair and gave him an insolent stare.

It seemed Oldfield thought he'd got his measure and could speak in a patronising manner without bringing any retribution on himself. Seeing as his alibi had fallen flat on its face and he was back in the frame, Rafferty wondered where he found the nerve.

'What relevance does it have? Adrienne had been dead for hours according to you. What difference does it make where I went?'

'It might not make any difference in that way. That being so, I don't understand why you didn't mention it, but told us you were at home all evening. Humour me. I'm curious as to why you thought we wouldn't be interested in *all* your movements.'

'As I said – I don't see the relevance. But if you must know, I went to see a friend.'

'I see. And would that be a male friend or a female one?'

'Female, as it happens.'

'And this lady's name?'

Oldfield balked a bit at disclosing this information, but eventually supplied it. He was reticent about answering their other questions and Rafferty had once again to remind him that this was a murder inquiry and that his alibi had gone the way of the dodo. He told him that a reluctance to answer police questions inevitably made him more interesting as a suspect.

Oldfield's lips thinned at this, but his reticence vanished. It was clear that once he'd decided to answer their questions more fully, he was keen to remove himself from their list of suspects. He'd lost his mistress; and if she had any sense he'd also lose his girlfriend. It was clear that he didn't want to be charged with murder and lose his freedom, too.

'Quite a busy man on the lady friend front,' said Rafferty when he finally let Oldfield go. 'I don't know how he ever found time to do any work. I wonder if he's got any more women stashed away?'

'I doubt we'll ever know. Not that it's relevant, any more than is where he went late on the evening of the murder, just as Mr Oldfield said.'

'I suppose I was just being nosy in questioning him about it. Though it might be significant that we found him out in another lie, or at least a failure to reveal something that might be of relevance. Oh well, let's have the girlfriend up now and see what she has to say.'

Diana Rexton had little to say. She seemed very subdued. Perhaps, finally, the shock of Oldfield's betrayal was starting to sink in. But Rafferty didn't allow that to influence him. She had lied for Oldfield's sake about him being at home all afternoon and evening of the murder and he wanted to hear her explain why.

Rafferty could have sworn Diana Rexford had told him the truth when she'd said that Oldfield hadn't left the flat after he had come home at four o'clock. He'd been convinced of her honesty about this vital matter, yet the course of their investigation had revealed that she must have lied. How could he have been so wrong about her? She must be a better liar than he would have given her credit for and – to lie for him in a murder investigation – must also love Oldfield to the point of obsession.

Furious that he'd been taken in by what he had regarded as her shining honesty, he knew in his heart that his fury was for himself and his own failure to pick up on the falsehood. Well, now he had her seated in a chair opposite him. He'd make her explain her lies.

'So, just to get to the point of this interview. I'd like to know why you lied about Gary being at home around five o'clock. You also didn't tell the truth about his second outing late that evening.'

'As to the latter, I don't see that it matters, except to me, where he went and who he saw. It can't have any relevance to the murder. Besides, I was in bed nursing a sick headache. I went to sleep early and didn't hear him go out.'

'And what about the earlier time? Your boyfriend has admitted he went out around five o'clock. Yet you said he was in with you for the entire evening.'

Diana Rexton blushed at this. 'I didn't lie,' she insisted, pink spots staining her cheeks after the blush had faded. 'I didn't know he'd gone out.'

'He said he went out for a Chinese takeaway and that he went to one close to the Staveleys' home.'

'I knew he was ordering a Chinese. I just assumed he'd ordered a home delivery meal from our local takeaway. I was in the bath,' she added hastily, 'so didn't realize he'd gone out.'

'No. Apparently the local Chinese restaurant didn't meet Mr Oldfield's exacting standards.'

'As I said, I was having a bath. I'd taken a fall on Benjy while I was exercising him and felt a bit stiff. I had a nice long soak. Thankfully, it eased my muscles. I live in fear of injury,' she told them. 'I need to stay fit to be considered by the Olympic selectors.'

Rafferty was surprised that the horse riding he had thought of as just a hobby turned out to be deadly serious. 'I'd give up riding Benjy, in that case, if I were you. He looks a bit too wayward to me to risk injury by riding him. Not that I know anything about horses.'

'I'll bear it in mind. But Benjy likes to get out. And as no one else will ride him it falls to me to exercise him.'

'You could always sell him and save your bones.'

'Sell him? I couldn't do that. As I told you before, I've had him from a foal. He's not used to anyone else. He'd hate to live with strangers.'

'OK, Ms Rexton, that'll be all for now. But keep yourself ready for any possible further questions that we might have.'

She gave an anxious smile and followed the uniformed officer who led her back downstairs.

Rafferty lolled back in the chair. 'So what do you think, Dafyd? Me I've always felt this had to be a man's crime, committed on the spur of the moment, which is indicated by the fact that the killer didn't use a weapon. Which, apart from Oldfield, seems to indicate John Staveley or Kyle as they both had strong reasons for wanting her dead. Either one of them could have been pushed too far by Adrienne and grabbed her around the throat in an attempt to shut her up – she seems to have been a provoking sort of woman. All it might have taken for her to die was a matter of seconds. It could have happened before her killer realized what they were doing. A tragic accident, when all is said and done. But murder none the less for that. Or manslaughter at least.'

'The boy, do you think more likely than the father? All those raging teenage hormones could tip the balance and make him lose control and attack her.'

'Perhaps. But I can't see Kyle managing to keep it a secret. I think he's the sort of kid who would have to blurt it out to someone and sooner rather than later. No, John Staveley seems the more likely of the two, given the marriage situation and her assorted lovers. He must surely have known about at least one of them. It would easily be enough to tip a man over the edge, particularly a man like John Staveley who strikes me as the brooding sort and who's already lost so much.'

'I suppose you're right,' said Llewellyn. 'It sounds like it would be a good idea to pin Mr Staveley down as to exactly where his wanderings took him that afternoon. He must have some idea of the times and the places he found himself. Surely he saw someone who knows him? He was wandering round for hours. He can't have walked around town all afternoon and part of the evening without someone he knows seeing him. If, that is, he *was* in town rather than rowing with and killing his wife.'

*   *   *

As it happened, one of his acquaintances *had* seen John Staveley in town. This fact was discovered by Gerry Hanks during routine questioning. Hanks returned to the station and brought it to Rafferty's attention just after Diana Rexton and Gary Oldfield had left. Staveley had been seen around three thirty, so it didn't put him out of the running for the murder, but at least it went partway to establishing his story.

Apart from Oldfield, who was newly restored to the suspect list, slowly, some suspects seemed to be slithering away from them. They'd think they'd got something firm on one of them and then it all turned to gossamer thread in their hands.

Why couldn't they find a time frame of more than fifteen minutes when Oldfield could have committed the crime? Why had John Staveley been seen, wandering in the town when they should have been able to place him at the scene murdering his wife? Why had neither David or Helen Ayling's cars shown up on CCTV near the Staveleys' around the right time?

This case was almost as much of a bitch as the victim. It was too bad and Bradley wasn't helping: he was being as bitchy as the case. The shining halo at Region that he was at such pains to cultivate must be getting seriously tarnished.

Rafferty was glad. He felt sour and not inclined to be charitable. He also had the worry of Abra, the wedding and honeymoon to contend with, not to mention the third estate which were starting to write vociferous editorials criticising the police in general and him in particular, which didn't help. Whichever way he looked, he had people on his back, badgering him. He was getting fed up with it.

At least interest in their two flats was continuing apace and, on the strength of this, they felt able to make an offer on the semi-detached that Abra had set her heart on. It was the only area where things were progressing satisfactorily and Rafferty was grateful for it. He touched wood and crossed his fingers to ensure this happy state of affairs continued.

As for the wedding – it was less than a week away and they were no nearer to knowing what to do – whether to cancel it or go through with the ceremony. Rafferty, at least, was determined it would go ahead. He wanted no postponement; he had a fear that if he let Abra slip through his fingers this time there wouldn't be another opportunity. She'd now had more than a taste of what disruption a policeman's job could cause to a private life and she didn't like it. Just as Sam Dally had said at the PM, Rafferty was sure she would easily find another partner to marry her. The thought had plagued him ever since Sam had made the comment. Now, added to that worry, was the suspicion that she was having an affair with John Staveley. What did she see in him that I can't supply? was Rafferty's thought. I make her laugh. I can't imagine that the morose man that Gary Oldfield described does that. He wondered, in typical male fashion, if Staveley had a bigger dick. But whatever he had, Abra must like it and had selected the man as her lover. Maybe she would want to replace me as a permanent fixture in her life? It would explain why she had said she wanted to postpone the wedding. Maybe she was working herself up to cancelling it altogether?

Rafferty thought of himself as a sad, forty-year-old git who worked unsocial hours – what chance did he have to find another partner? Besides, he didn't want anyone else. Abra was the only girl he wanted to marry and he'd played the field enough in his younger days to know the difference between real love and infatuation for a pretty face. Or at least, he'd played the field until his then girlfriend, Angie, fell pregnant only to miscarry shortly after their hasty marriage. They'd certainly repented at leisure and it was a merciful release for both of them when death rather than divorce had ended their union. Divorce would have been out of the question – at least as far as his ma was concerned – as they were both Catholics. Not that the very lapsed Rafferty would have objected. He'd have welcomed divorce, but he was reluctant to upset his mother, especially as he was the favourite of her six children and would have been the first in the immediate family to permanently split from his partner.

But all that was over and now he had new problems to tackle. Not least of which, was yet another marital situation. Abra thought they should postpone as she didn't want him disappearing halfway through the reception, leaving her abandoned. Or so she said. She had told him that would be mortifying and he had told her it wouldn't happen. He could take the evening off from the case – so could Llewellyn for that matter. Even Superintendent Bradley couldn't deny him that, whatever else he might begrudge.

No, it wasn't the wedding or Bradley that was causing him

most angst, it was the investigation, not to mention Abra's possible part in it. If only he could get a handle on one of the suspects, but there was nothing to single any of them out. Any one of them could have done it. That was the problem.

Bradley seemed of the opinion that he should just select the most likely and charge them and wait for the evidence to catch up. But Rafferty didn't want to do that. He'd done so in his last investigation and it had ended in tears all round, not least Bradley's as his dead cert had proved to be anything but.

Oh well, he thought, at least things seemed to be going well on the house front. Their offer on the semi in town had been accepted this afternoon – Abra had rung to tell him. Now it was just a matter of the sale of their two flats progressing apace. It complicated matters that they had two flats to sell as it involved them in two separate chains with all that that entailed. But he wouldn't look on the black side where that was concerned at least. The house business was going well; hopefully, it would continue to do so. What he needed was something new on the murder front.

To Rafferty's surprise, he got something new on the murder front the very next day – at least he thought he did – as Mrs Staveley Senior was attacked in her own home. Someone had tried to strangle her, just like her daughter-in-law.

THIRTEEN

When Rafferty went to see Edith Staveley at her son's home, where she had gone after the assault on her, she tried to appear her usual strong-minded self, but it was clear that it was an effort of will and didn't quite succeed. Although her spine still didn't rest against the back of her son's more comfortable armchair, it sagged a little from her former straight stance. Unsurprisingly, the attack had shaken her. Rafferty asked her how she was feeling.

Her voice was croaky and difficult to understand as her throat had been badly bruised. But she insisted she was OK and could talk.

'Have you seen a doctor?' he asked.

'My mother's GP has been to see her,' John Staveley told him. 'He's given her sleeping tablets and some tranquillizers as a short-term measure.'

'I won't take them, so he was wasting his time. I've no patience with people who are reliant on pills. It's different if one is in extreme pain. Otherwise, I see little reason to medicate.'

'Even so, Mother,' said Staveley, 'he must think you need them. Please try them, at least.'

Edith Staveley's lips firmed and her back regained a little more of her previous upright stance as she said, 'No. I told you I won't take them and I meant it. I'll get through any sleepless nights with that old standby, cocoa. You know how much I dislike taking tablets.'

'My mother rarely takes even a painkiller for a headache,' Staveley told Rafferty. 'I tell her it doesn't mean she's being weak, but she thinks otherwise.'

Rafferty, as one who had to have recourse to painkillers regularly, nodded as if he was in total agreement, and said, 'Can you tell me what happened, Mrs Staveley?'

'Certainly. I've lost my confidence, not my memory. Someone rang the front door bell and when I answered the door there was a man in a balaclava standing there. He forced me backwards into the hall, slammed the door shut, and demanded to know where I kept my valuables. I wasn't going to tell him, I can assure you of that. Anyway, I managed to get away from him and ran into the kitchen. I'd been rolling pastry for a steak and kidney pie, which I was making for John and Kyle, when he rang the bell. So, when he put his hands round my throat I picked up the rolling pin and hit him with it. I managed to hit him several times even though he was trying to choke me. I almost blacked out, but thankfully, he let go and ran off, back out the front door. I ran after him and banged it shut behind him. That's when I called the police and John.'

'Thank you. Your description is very clear. Can you tell me any more about this man? For instance, was he tall or short? Fat or thin?'

'He was tall and well built. About John's height. I was lucky to fight him off.'

He agreed with her, though he wouldn't say so. To agree might only add stronger ammunition to her future nightmares.

'Did he have any distinguishing marks? Tattoos, that kind of thing.'

'Not that I noticed, though he had a long-sleeved jacket and gloves on, so I wouldn't have seen.'

He'd come prepared then, was Rafferty's thought. The gloves in June told him that, not to mention the balaclava.

'Did you recognize his voice? Or did it have any kind of noticeable accent?' he asked.

'No. I don't think so. But he didn't say much – just the demand for valuables.'

'It must have been an unpleasant experience for you.'

'Yes. I've always felt so safe in that house, even after my husband died and I lived alone. I never shall again. My son said I can stay with him for as long as I like – until he manages to sell the house, anyway.'

'That sounds like a good idea. At least till you get over the worst of the shock. And when you go back home don't answer the door unless the chain's on.'

She nodded and he left her then with best wishes for a speedy recovery. But she wasn't a young woman and he wondered how long it would take her to get over the attack.

Some people never got over such an experience and it blighted the rest of their lives.

He wondered how – or if – this attack impinged on their murder case. Were they connected? Or was it a coincidence and this just a random attack by a young thug on a woman who was alone and vulnerable? Did it mean that Adrienne, too, had been attacked by a stranger who just turned up at her door and overpowered her?

The thought was a worrying one. If this was a stranger killing, their chances of catching the killer reduced proportionately. But would Adrienne have opened the door to a stranger when she had the spy hole to check on the identity of visitors?

At least there was a certain satisfaction in knowing Mrs Staveley had successfully fought off her attacker and that he hadn't managed to steal anything. She was a brave woman to have fought off the assailant – brave or foolhardy – as he could easily have seized a knife from the kitchen rack and stabbed her. Perhaps her attack with the rolling pin had stunned him: he wouldn't have expected an elderly woman to fight back, even best him.

He walked back to the car, returned to the station and updated Llewellyn.

'An attempted strangulation,' the Welshman mused. 'Think it's got any connection to our murder?'

'I don't know. It's a bit of a coincidence that two women in the same family should be attacked in a similar way. But John Staveley said there was nothing missing after Adrienne was killed, whereas the man who made the attack on Mrs Staveley Senior was clearly after money or jewellery. Anyway, I made some notes for what they're worth. I'll get them typed up. By the way,' he said as Llewellyn made for the door, 'you weren't going anywhere near the canteen were you?'

'I wasn't, but I could.'

'Good man. Get me some tea and a bacon butty, will you? My stomach thinks my throat's been cut.' Rafferty put his hand in his pocket for some cash to give to Llewellyn and wondered at his appetite. He'd already eaten one breakfast this morning – a large fry-up. He shouldn't be hungry again, but he was.

While Llewellyn was gone, Rafferty batted his two-fingered

way through his interview with Mrs Staveley Senior. His mind niggled at him as he typed. He was familiar with that particular niggle. It meant his mind was trying to point him in a new direction. Was it something he wasn't doing? Something was making him edgy. He just wished he knew what it was, though it must surely have something to do with this latest attack. He ran through the events as described by Edith Staveley, but nothing leapt out at him.

Although it was a short enough interview that he was typing up, he was still at it when Llewellyn returned. He took a break from typing to eat his butty, slapping his lips as he tucked in. He made short work of the sandwich, sipped at his tea, then returned to his typing.

'Can you arrange a house-to-house round Mrs Staveley's home, Dafyd?' he asked as he finished typing up the interview. 'Someone might have noticed this thug arrive or leave. They might have even seen him without his balaclava and be able to give a more detailed description than Mrs Staveley was able to supply. Also, check up for similar assaults during the course of robberies. It could be that matey-boy makes a habit of these assaults. Check with the other police stations in the district, too, as he might have spread his attacks over a wider area than just Elmhurst and it mightn't have got on the system yet.

'It's a shame her house is set well back from the road, though. Means it's less likely anyone noticed anything.'

'Let's wait and see. I'll go and get the house-to-house organized.'

The house-to-house didn't take long. Mrs Staveley Senior's home was in an expensive area of Elmhurst with each house nestled in a large plot, so there weren't too many neighbours to interview. Only one had seen anything – a man parked in a car outside Mrs Staveley's house. This neighbour had noticed it particularly because all of the houses in the road had spacious drives with no need for visitors to park on the street. There were no shops in the immediate vicinity so that wouldn't have been a reason for his presence and there was nothing else on that stretch of road but private houses. The thug had been without his balaclava at the time – if, that was, this man had been the thug who had attacked Edith Staveley – though the neighbour had been too far away to provide them with much of a description.

He hadn't taken the registration number, though it seemed probable the car had been stolen, so even if the neighbour had taken the number it wouldn't have gained them anything. But the question was – was it just an opportunistic attack or had it a connection to the murder? On the surface, the two women were very different: Adrienne Staveley was a woman with more men friends than morals. Whereas Mrs Staveley Senior had struck Rafferty as a very upright woman, a bit like an older, female version of Llewellyn. The two women had nothing in common so it was no wonder they hadn't had a loving relationship, even allowing for the usual mother-in-law difficulties. Yet was there a connection between the two crimes? Why would there be? Two very different women with two very similar injuries, in two widely separate parts of town; two assaults one of which had been taken to the ultimate. It was fortunate that the second attack hadn't had a similar result.

Another difference between the two women – Rafferty couldn't imagine Adrienne making pastry and having a rolling pin to hand with which to assail her attacker. Maybe that was why she was dead . . .

He had the description of the thug, such as it was, circulated in the area. It wasn't a lot to go on. Edith Staveley had offered a reward leading to the capture of her attacker, which might throw up a few leads although, inevitably, it would also throw up a lot of time-wasters looking to get their own back on an ex-husband or former boyfriend as well as those simply hoping to get their hands on the money. It would take a hell of a lot of man-hours to sift the results, but the information coming in had slowed to a trickle, so it would give the team something to do.

They already had the task of questioning the people on the list of friends and acquaintances that John Staveley had supplied. He had been able to recall some of the streets where his wandering had taken him on the day of the murder, so something else might come of it to support his story.

Maybe, as he said to Llewellyn, as their next step, they should make time to re-interview David Ayling in the presence of his wife and bring up his obsession with Adrienne and the fact that, apparently, unbeknown to that same wife, he had been in the habit of dropping in at The White Farmhouse several times a week. It would set the lion amongst the wildebeests and stir them up, stimulating distrust between them. This was something that Rafferty often felt guilty about, particularly for those amongst the suspects who turned out to have nothing to do with a murder, but it was an essential part of an investigation. There was nothing like witnessing a good row for throwing up new evidence. But that would have to wait till this evening.

Rafferty made arrangements for Llewellyn to pick him up at eight o'clock and drive them to the Aylings' house, and then he went home. All he was doing was supervising a lot of routine stuff and the team hardly needed his input for this. It was an early end to his day for a change, and, as a surprise for Abra, he popped into Sainsbury's and bought ingredients for their evening meal: lamb's liver cooked with apple, bacon and fried onions with mashed potato and runner beans. He even provided a pudding, though this was a creation of Mr Kipling rather than himself.

He was looking forward to seeing David and Helen Ayling this evening. It should liven things up once he'd revealed Ayling's obsession with Adrienne Staveley. It was always interesting to stir the brew and see what happened.

Abra was upset that he had to go out again that evening. They'd enjoyed a lovely dinner and had laughed a lot and teased each other even more than usual. He had left it late to break the news, knowing she wouldn't like it and reluctant to spoil the part of what remained of the evening that they *could* be together with arguments or recriminations.

After promising her he wouldn't be above an hour, he put on his jacket and was ready to slip out the door when Llewellyn rang the bell. He was on time, as always, spot on eight o'clock.

The Aylings' home looked even more attractive at night with the lamps lit and a fire sparking in the grate.

Helen Ayling wasn't quite as forgiving of her partner as had been Diana Rexton.

As soon as Rafferty had broken the glad tidings of her husband's regular visits to Adrienne, she turned on him. At that moment she had a look of her mother, the stern and upright Mrs Staveley Senior.

'What were you thinking of, visiting that woman? I wouldn't have thought she was your type.'

The Adrienne Staveleys of this world were every man's type, as far as Rafferty was concerned. It was clear from her diary that Adrienne had liked sex, unlike a lot of wives who generally pleaded a headache to get out of it.

'Why did you visit her? Were you having an affair with her?'

'No. Of course I wasn't. She'd never have looked at me that way. I knew that, an attractive woman like her. I'm paunchy and balding. Only a mother and a long-term wife could love me.'

'I'm not sure I do love you any more. I thought I knew you. Now I discover I don't know you at all. When I think of all those evenings you said you were working late. Why did you find it necessary to lie if you weren't hopeful of getting into her bed?'

'Because I knew you wouldn't like me visiting her. I told you – I knew there was no hope of getting into her bed. That wasn't why I went to see her.'

And if he believed that he was more deluded than Rafferty had thought. Of course he had wanted to get into her bed. And even though he knew her to be a selfish bitch, Rafferty thought he, too, would have given way to temptation as well a few years ago. Before he met Abra.

Either Helen Ayling was a very good actress or she really hadn't known of her husband's visits to Adrienne – which removed her reason to kill her. Unless, that was, the big sister syndrome of protecting her little brother was more developed than usual and she had killed Adrienne for her brother's sake rather than her own.

Either way, she didn't seem about to confess, so he left them to their mutual recriminations, which had developed into simmering silences on both sides, rather than the interesting spat that had happened earlier, said good night and led Llewellyn from the room.

Christ, thought Rafferty, as he lay in bed that night, suddenly wide awake. John Staveley had his house up for sale. How had he missed Edith Staveley's reference to this? It could be important.

They'd thought all along that Adrienne Staveley had known her attacker. But supposing she hadn't and had only let them in because she was expecting *someone*? Someone like a possible house purchaser.

Rafferty felt an urge to get up and dress and drive himself over to John Staveley's house to question him on the matter. But it was three o'clock in the morning. No way he could go waking the household up, particularly when it contained Staveley's recently assaulted mother who would surely receive another unwanted shock if he started hammering on the front door at this hour.

Beside him, Abra stirred in her sleep and he sat still and quiet so as not to disturb her. She quickly turned over and subsided and Rafferty sank back against his pillows to think things through.

Why hadn't Staveley had a 'For Sale' sign posted on his gate? Because of the lack of such a sign it had been a mere fluke that he'd found out about the sale, yet the estate agents – whoever they were, which was something else he would have to ask Staveley – could have sent Adrienne's murderer to her door.

With such new possibilities opening up, he found he couldn't go back to sleep. So, rather than sit in the dark for the rest of the night waiting for the dawn, he got up and went along the hall to the kitchen to make himself some tea.

Once the kettle boiled and he made the tea, he sat at the kitchen table nursing his warming mug and listening to rain spattering against the window. The weathermen had promised a dry and bright day so it seemed likely that the rain would be in for the duration.

He sipped his tea and felt an almost overwhelming urge to ring Llewellyn and get his take on the latest turn of events, but knowing his luck his wife Maureen would pick up the phone. She'd probably tear him off a strip before she disconnected or more probably pull the jack from the wall in case he was foolhardy enough to try his luck a second time.

He had drunk three mugs of tea by the time the first rosy fingers of the new day showed over the horizon. At least the rain had stopped, so perhaps he had been unfair to the weathermen. It was still early; too early to take up Abra's tea. Instead, he decided to make himself a fry up: it would set him up for the day and enable him to make an early start once the morning was properly begun.

By half past six he couldn't wait any longer. He made more tea and brought Abra in a cup. She was very sleepy and he had to shake her to get her to wake up.

She finally opened her eyes. But it was only to glare at him. 'What's the matter with you?' she demanded. 'Is the flat on fire?'

'No. I am. Something about the case struck me in the middle of the night.'

'What?' She sat up. 'Do you know who did it?'

'Not exactly,' he said, sorry to disappoint her. 'It's just that I've found out that the Staveleys had their house up for sale, so Mrs Staveley might have had any number of strangers turning up on her doorstep when she was alone in the house. Perhaps the opportunity was just too much for some sick individual. It throws the possibilities – and the potential suspects – wide open.'

'Oh God, no.' Abra sat back against her pillows and gave them a thump. 'That'll make you even further from finding a solution.'

'Not necessarily. The house has no "For Sale" sign on the gate so they wouldn't have had just anyone popping in off the street on the off-chance. Not that that would be likely in any case as the house is in a short cul-de-sac. No. The estate agent would have sent any prospective buyers along and would have got their details.'

'Surely no one would be stupid enough to commit murder when any such possible suspects must be severely limited and would soon be discovered?'

Rafferty felt an uneasy stirring at her words. This had, of course, occurred to him, too. But he had brushed the thought aside with the explanation that a person would have to be mentally unstable to commit such a murder when their name and address could be quickly discovered. There again, there were plenty of mentally unstable individuals wandering the streets. The Care in the Community programme had seen to that, sending vast swathes of the vulnerable and possibly dangerous out from the old mental hospitals, many of which had been tarted up and sold as expensive apartments. One of these probably homeless and wandering souls could have seen the house advert in the estate agent's window and recognized the place. Who knew what had been going through their mind when – if – they had knocked on Adrienne's door? The thought was a worrying one, bringing with it, as it did, the possibility of an attack by a stranger.

But Rafferty didn't want to think about that. It was easier to seize on the supposition that the estate agent had sent Adrienne's murderer to her house. He had waited for so long for answers in the case and now he had one. Or at least the possibility of one. He wasn't going to lose hold of it easily.

It was eight a.m. when Rafferty presented himself at John Staveley's door. It was early, yes, but he couldn't wait any longer. He might already have waited too long. Even now the maniac that Rafferty had conjured up in his mind and hadn't been able to forget about, might have attacked another woman.

Staveley had clearly still been in bed when Rafferty knocked as he opened the door in his dressing gown with his hair standing on end and sleep in his eyes.

'Inspector. What do you want? It's barely eight o'clock.'

'Yes. I'm sorry about disturbing you so early, sir, but something your mother said yesterday suddenly struck me.'

'Who is it, John?' Edith Staveley's newly quavery voice floated down the stairs.

'It's all right, Mother. It's Inspector Rafferty. Go back to bed.'

'What does he want at this time of the morning?'

The voice and its owner descended the stairs, audibly muttering about the thoughtlessness of early morning visitors as she did so.

'I don't know, Mother. I was just about to ask him.' Staveley turned back to Rafferty. 'Inspector?'

'It's just something your mother said when I questioned her after she was assaulted. It didn't hit me until later. I understand you have your house up for sale?'

'Yes. What of it?'

'It's just that I wondered if someone might have come to the door purporting to be interested in buying the place.'

'It's unlikely. As you'll have seen, we didn't have an estate agent's sign up. Adrienne wouldn't have one as she didn't want our neighbours to know we were selling the place and downsizing until they saw the removals van.'

'I see. I wanted to ask you for the name of your estate

agent. It's a possibility that they sent your wife's killer along to see the house.' Though the more he thought about it, the more Rafferty became reluctantly convinced that it had been an opportunist and not an appointee sent along by the estate agents who had done the deed.

'Well, come in, Inspector. Come in,' said Edith Staveley as she descended the bend in the bottom of the stairs. 'It's too chilly at this time of the morning to stand around on the doorstep. I'll put the kettle on while John looks for the estate agent's particulars. I've forgotten their name for the minute.'

'And me.' John Staveley went into the kitchen, closely followed by Edith Staveley, with Rafferty bringing up the rear. It was a generously sized kitchen, with granite worktops and a dark green Aga sitting squarely in what had clearly been the farmhouse's original fireplace.

Mrs Staveley seized the kettle from under her son's nose and told him to go and find the agent's particulars. Staveley, as though, like Rafferty, he was used to obeying orders, turned and went out.

'Sit down, Inspector,' she told him as she got the mugs out and put them by the teapot on top of the Aga. 'I don't suppose my son will be long. He's pretty organized when it comes to paperwork.'

She was right and Staveley was soon back. He sat down at the kitchen table beside Rafferty and handed him the sheet of paper that had the house details and estate agent's particulars on it.

Rafferty froze as he took in the name of the estate agent. Blythe's. Surely Nigel couldn't be mixed up in this killing? And why hadn't he mentioned that he was the agent dealing with the sale of a house where a woman had been murdered? The death had had wall-to-wall coverage in the local press and television.

This was Abra all over again, he thought, only this time, it was his cousin's fingerprints that lay heavy at the scene. Suddenly, it struck him that this murder was too close to home for comfort.

Furious with Nigel and his failure to communicate this latest information, he yanked his mobile from his pocket and dialled his home number. Nigel was due to have a few questions put

to him and Rafferty intended to get some straight answers
out of him as soon as possible. He didn't care if he woke him
from his beauty sleep. Becoming a bit plainer would do him the
world of good.

FOURTEEN

Nigel wasn't best pleased to be woken up. He told Rafferty so in no uncertain terms. 'What the hell do you want, Joe? It's my day off. I had a late night and was sleeping it off.'

Rafferty excused himself to John Staveley and his mother and went into the hall, shutting the kitchen door behind him. 'I'm investigating the murder of Adrienne Staveley, as I told you days ago. And what do I find? That you're the agent acting for her and her husband in their house sale. Why didn't you tell me that you're the agent? I had to find it out for myself. It's made me feel a right plonker.'

'So what's new? And so what if I am the agent? That woman's murder is nothing to do with me. I barely knew her – I only met her the once. I mostly dealt with her husband.'

'Even so, you should have told me about it. For all I know you made Adrienne Staveley an appointment with death.' Rafferty would have threatened to charge him with impeding an investigation if he'd thought the threat would have any effect. But he'd already threatened Nigel once during this case, over the misappropriated honeymoon payment and it had had no effect. His cousin knew the situation *vis-à-vis* the station and how unwilling Rafferty was to have one of his family pop up there as a suspect or witness in case it rebounded on him. Nigel also knew that Rafferty wasn't flavour of the month or even the decade with Superintendent Bradley, who would be delighted to have a reason to suspend him. 'Tell me about Mrs Staveley. What did you think of her?'

'She was an attractive woman. Flirtatious, too. I could have got in there if I had the time. But I'm overburdened with women in my life at the moment. There's only so much one man can do to satisfy the fair sex.'

Nigel's words sounded as if he was boasting, but Rafferty didn't doubt his popularity with the female of the species. His cousin was something of a ladies' man and always had a girlfriend or three on the go. He didn't know how Nigel found the energy. 'Go on. What else?'

'She dressed like she wanted to attract a man. You know, low-slung top and tight trousers. I got the impression she wasn't keen on selling the farmhouse. Well, it was more than an impression, actually. She told me as much. Seemed it was her old man who was driving the sale.'

'Do you remember anything else?'

'No. That's about it. Will you have to call me as a witness, coz? Only I'll be happy to make myself available.'

'I bet you would. But I doubt it will be necessary.' Nigel preening from the witness box as he toyed with the possibility of mentioning his relationship to the senior investigating officer was the stuff of nightmares. 'Thanks for the info. You'd better get yourself along to your office sharpish, as I want a list of all the people you sent to view the house.'

'None of my clients would have killed her.' Nigel put on his superior voice. 'I only deal with respectable people in the upper income bracket.'

'Go on, Nigel. We both know you'd deal with Jack the Ripper if you thought there was a profit in it. Anyway, rise and shine. And don't bother to put the coffee on. I want that information in the next fifteen minutes. I'm on my mobile. Ring me.' Rafferty shut his phone and returned it to his pocket as something very welcome occurred to him. It was as if a bright light flickered on in his brain. He could have rung Nigel back there and then, but he decided against it. He had his cousin's unwilling co-operation for now. He didn't want to antagonise him by ringing back immediately, with yet more questions. He went back into the kitchen, sat down and said, 'Tell me, Mr Staveley, did you by any chance have a young woman by the name of Miss Kearney view the house? Young, late twenties, attractive and with long hair, probably worn in a plait?'

Staveley shrugged. 'I don't know. I only dealt with the agent. Adrienne dealt with most of those who came to view. As I told you, I was out of the house all day. I mostly only saw them when she brought them into my study to see the room, but I don't remember a young woman. All the people I saw were middle-aged couples. Why are you particularly interested in this young woman, anyway? Do you think she—?'

'No reason,' Rafferty interrupted. 'Just something I heard,' he said non-committally. He drained his tea. 'Never mind. I'm sure Mr Blythe at the estate agents will be able to tell me what I want to know. Thanks for your help and thank you for the tea,' he said to Edith Staveley. 'I'll get back to the station now.'

Rafferty got back on to Nigel as soon as he had closed the door behind him. He found he couldn't wait, after all, seeing as Staveley had been unable to help him. He needed the information and he needed it now. And to hell with antagonising Nigel.

At first, just to be awkward, his cousin said he couldn't recall the name of every person that asked for house details, but Rafferty pressed him and his memory soon improved. It turned out that Nigel *did* remember Abra requesting details of the Staveley's house and making an appointment to view. He felt a huge surge of relief as he got in the car and started it up. No wonder her prints were in every room, even Staveley's bedroom. She wasn't having an affair with him. She hadn't murdered Adrienne. All she had done was view a house way above their price range. She was just being nosey and he had her marked down as a near adulteress or a murderer. Thank God and cowardice that he hadn't questioned her about it. Now he wouldn't have to do so at all. He'd been dreading doing it: terrified of what he'd find out and terrified of what would happen to their marriage plans. Terrified, too, that he might have to lock her up.

Llewellyn's check of the neighbouring police stations about other burglaries with violence similar to that used on Edith Staveley didn't bear fruit. Perhaps any other victims hadn't got away from the man as had Mrs Staveley, when she ran to her kitchen and prompted the would-be thief to become angry, chase after her and put his hands round her neck.

There had been two opportunistic thefts in the surrounding villages, but neither had been violent. Both the victims were women, which made Rafferty think the thief had studied the houses and their occupants, noting when the woman of the house was there alone. It was a cowardly crime.

Rafferty guessed that the thief had a drug habit and had used the proceeds of his crimes to buy his latest supplies. If he was the same man as had attacked and killed Adrienne they would surely already have his prints if he was caught committing another crime. Rafferty was willing to bet that if none of their current suspects had killed her, then one of the so far unidentified sets of prints in Adrienne's kitchen and on her front door belonged to her killer as he had clearly not worn gloves when he strangled her: his finger marks were round her neck as Sam had told him. He had been hopeful of getting DNA evidence from any sweat left behind, but Sam had told him that the neck wasn't a very fertile area for getting DNA. Rafferty could only hope they got lucky and caught the bastard.

It was the night of Rafferty's stag do. Abra was having her hen night at the same time and they were both getting ready. Abra looked very fetching in a short, low-cut and sleeveless white dress and a short and frivolous-looking veil. She wore a red letter 'L' on her back, and had put a white, blue beribboned lacy garter on her leg. This latter had stirred Rafferty's libido to the extent that he had wanted to take it off again. But he had restrained the impulse. There was no time before Llewellyn arrived, unfortunately.

'You're no learner,' Rafferty told her, in reference to the beginner's sign. 'In fact, I reckon you could teach me a thing or two.'

'And the rest. That Catholic schooling of yours has left you decidedly conscience-ridden about doing naughty things. I only hope getting married and having the Church's blessing on the conjugals will remove some of your hang-ups.'

'We'll just have to practise a lot. Anyway, enough dirty talk. You're all ready, but what should I wear?' he asked as he opened the wardrobe door and peered inside. 'One of my new suits?'

'No. You don't want to ruin it or worse – lose it.'

'Dafyd's in charge. He won't let me be tied naked to a lamppost. You know what a stickler he is for propriety. Besides, it wouldn't do for a copper to be caught in such a compromising position. I think even Mickey and Patrick Sean would stop short at that.'

'Even so. Your brothers might get a bit boisterous and ignore Dafyd. Wear something older that you don't mind getting ruined.'

That meant his old faithful brown suit that was decidedly shabby. His other old suits were even shabbier. 'I've got to wear something reasonably smart to get into the clubs.'

Abra had lost interest in what he wore. She had been admiring herself in her wardrobe mirror and now she said, 'Talking of clubs – which ones are you going to?'

'I don't know. Dafyd's organized it. Knowing him it'll be the Liberal Club.'

Abra laughed and turned to face him. 'He's not that bad. Only we're going to Cynbyn and I don't want to bump into you and the rest of the stag night crew.'

'Don't worry. I'll make sure we don't go there. There's plenty of others to choose from.'

'Try not to get too wasted.'

'It's my stag do, sweetheart. I'm supposed to get wasted. It's traditional.'

'Even so.'

'Don't worry,' he said again. 'Dafyd will look after me and see I get home OK.'

'Thank God for him as he'll be the only sensible one amongst you.' Outside a car gave a long blast on its horn.

'Anyway, that'll be my cab. I'm off. Have a good time.'

'And you.' Rafferty came over and kissed her. 'And don't you drink too much, either. I don't want some Lothario taking advantage of you.'

'This is strictly a girls' night out. No fraternization allowed.'

'Glad to hear it. Even so, just you be careful. A few drinks and you might forget the no-fraternization rule.'

Abra left and Rafferty continued to get ready, deciding, after all, to wear one of the smart Italian suits that he'd bought before he met Abra, sure that Dafyd would take care that nothing happened to it or him. The decision didn't take long. Llewellyn was knocking on the door five minutes later to collect him.

The Welshman looked smart, but then he always did. He was as dapper as Beau Brummell, though without the flamboyance.

'Are you ready?' he asked.

Rafferty nodded.

'Shall we go then? I'll pick up your two brothers on the way to the pub.'

Llewellyn didn't drink, so had volunteered to drive the three Rafferty brothers. The rest of the party were making their own transport arrangements.

Collecting Mickey and Patrick Sean didn't take long as they both lived in Elmhurst. Within fifteen minutes, they were in the Red Lion on Elmhurst's High Street. This, of course, was Llewellyn's choice and was the favoured pub of him and Maureen, his wife. It catered for what Rafferty called 'the cappuccino crowd' – middle-class intellectuals from the local college – and normally Rafferty steered well clear. The Red Lion was a smallish pub, with leather banquettes and a restaurant that had a Michelin star and that went in for fresh flowers on the tables. The décor was muted and could, he supposed, be described as stylish, with none of the garish décor often sported by the town's more utilitarian pubs. Its pale green walls featured photographs and paintings of Elmhurst and surrounds in centuries past, with more modern watercolours and oils by local artists which were for sale.

Rafferty's favourite pub was the Black Swan on the River Tiffey to the north of the town. It was a comfortable, down-to-earth hostelry without the pretensions of the Red Lion, which was also the favoured haunt of several of his superiors, including Superintendent Bradley – which was another reason to drink elsewhere.

The others in the party had beaten them to it and were already several drinks ahead, judging by the noise emanating from their table and the uproarious way they greeted Rafferty's arrival.

'So what are you having, Joe?' Mickey, one of his younger brothers, asked once the din of greetings had died down.

Rafferty raised his voice above the hubbub emanating from their table. 'I'll start off with an Adnam's Bitter and work my way up.'

'OK.' Mickey turned to Dafyd, put his mouth to his ear and shouted, 'Dafyd, what about you? What can I get you?'

Llewellyn shouted back, his expression pained. 'I'll have a pineapple juice, please.'

Rafferty grimaced. Poor Dafyd, it was going to be a long night for him. Rafferty guessed that the rowdiness of the stag night boys was already something of a torment to him; a torment that could only increase as the night wore on. But at least it was only once in a lifetime. Or twice, in his case.

The drinks were soon in and, several pints later, Rafferty felt nicely relaxed and ready to enjoy the remainder of the night. He soon became as raucous as the rest as he shouted to be heard. He had learned to drink bitter – rather than lager, which his contemporaries drank – from one of his uncles on his mother's side. Rafferty soon found he preferred it to the lager he had drunk with his friends.

They decided on a kitty and gave it to Llewellyn to look after.

The conversation didn't take long to turn smutty. It was something that Rafferty had expected, but by now he was past caring.

'So, have you got your stock of strawberry-flavoured condoms in for the honeymoon?' Mickey shouted, drawing several disapproving looks from the pub's other patrons.

'Abra doesn't like strawberry,' Rafferty replied, deadpan. 'She prefers tequila-flavoured ones. And banana. She likes a bit of variety.'

'Tequila? I didn't know you could get tequila-flavoured johnnies.'

'Joke. But perhaps some enterprising condom manufacturer makes them and the pub landlords in Elmhurst think their customers get through enough alcohol in the usual manner without them resorting to other means.' Rafferty stood up. 'My turn to get the drinks in.' He turned to Llewellyn and shouted, 'Give me some of the kitty money, Dafyd. Another pineapple juice for you, is it?'

Llewellyn's lips turned down. 'No thanks. I'll have a coffee.'

'Coffee it is. Same as before for the rest of you?'

They chorused their agreement and Rafferty walked over to the bar and consulted his list of drinks before he gave the beginning of the order to the barman. He decided to move to shorts and ordered a large Jameson's for himself. He preferred the Irish whiskey to Scotch; He found it smoother than its northern brother. Usually, he had Jameson's Triple Reserved whiskey – they kept it for him in the Black Swan and the Railway Arms. But he could only get the ordinary Jameson in the Red Lion and he was lucky to get that given the patrons' preferences, amongst which such specialized Irish whiskey still didn't feature, as his swift, assessing glance over the optics had already told him.

While he waited for the drinks to be served, and with the chance to observe the stag night boys in a more objective way, he decided to suggest they make a move when they'd drunk this round. Their noisy party was getting those mutterings of disapproval, which the British do so well, from the cappuccino crowd. He didn't want them to be asked to leave this early in the proceedings. It would be embarrassing if the landlord called the police.

In spite of Rafferty's misgivings about their rowdy behaviour, the others refused to leave the pub till closing time. They told him they didn't want to waste valuable drinking time traipsing between various bars. After a few more drinks he was past worrying if they disturbed the coffee aficionados or even if his uniformed colleagues were called in.

At closing time, they headed for the Scorpio Club. Llewellyn drove; the others in the party decided to walk, as it wasn't that far. Nigel, because the night was drizzly and he was, as usual, wearing one of his snazzy, made-to-measure suits, opted to wait for a taxi. He arrived at the Scorpio Club last, and was in a bad mood when he got there.

'You finally made it, then?' said Rafferty, as he downed his second whiskey.

'Damn taxi was late picking me up. I shan't use that firm again.'

'Never mind, Nige.' Rafferty stood up. 'Have a drink.'

'I'll have a large brandy.'

'Coming up. I'll get some money from Dafyd's kitty.'

The drink soon coaxed Nigel out of his ill-humour.

The night wore on and grew hazy. It was three in the morning before they staggered out of the last club. Quite early, really. But Rafferty was forty and not so up to such long hours as he'd once been. The others were around the same age and didn't make any objections to the relatively early end to their clubbing. Besides, unwisely, earlier in the evening, nicely lubricated and feeling hail-fellow-well-met, Rafferty had said they could all come back to his place. They didn't need a second invitation. He had thought they might have forgotten after their alcohol intake, but not a bit of it. The prospect of more, free, drink, was way too attractive for that. Abra was staying in her own place for the night, so they wouldn't disturb her.

They put some music on when they reached his flat and Rafferty brought out the booze.

'So, are you ready to be an old married man again?' Nigel asked as he sat down on the settee beside him.

'I certainly am. More than ready. There's no shotgun aspect to this marriage, unlike my first one.'

'Yeah. I remember. I always thought it was funny that you got caught like that, only for Angie's bun in the over to fall out a few months after you got hitched.'

Rafferty had always thought Angie's 'miscarriage' a bit suspect, too. Not that he was going to tell Nigel that. It was clear his cousin already thought him enough of a fool for getting caught by the pregnancy bogey in the first place. To admit to being duped by Angie with a fake pregnancy wouldn't be a wise move. He'd think him an even bigger fool if he confessed to his suspicions. Nigel was the sort of bloke – cousin or no cousin – who would take great delight in reminding him of such an unwise revelation. 'Yes, well, that's a long time ago, now. Water under the bridge.'

'If you say so. Abra not pregnant, is she?'

'No.' Rafferty's reply was curt. Nigel could be straight to the jugular at times and drink made him worse. It was probably brought about because of all the crawling he felt he had to do to his high-flying agency clientele. He liked to loosen the guard on his tongue on the rare occasions when he deigned to socialize with family and he tended to revert to his Jerry Kelly persona. Perhaps, too, he was getting his own back for Rafferty's brusqueness on the phone when he'd demanded the list of people who had viewed the Staveley house. They were still checking them out. A couple of them lived in Elmhurst, but most on the list lived miles away and he had sent the team out to do preliminary interviews. If he thought it necessary from the results of the preliminaries, he would see them himself.

Nigel lost interest in the subject, lounged back on Rafferty's settee, turned to Llewellyn and asked, 'So where are the dancing girls, then, Dafyd?'

'Dancing girls? There are no dancing girls.'

'I thought there wouldn't be.' He grinned, revealing his expensively capped American teeth – image was all with Nigel. 'Just as well I ordered some entertainment. Should be here soon.'

'What did you order?' Rafferty asked.

'A stripper. She said she'd come around four.'

At his words, as if on cue, there was a ring at the door. Rafferty wondered how Nigel had known he would be stupid enough to let them all loose on his drinks cupboard. But then Nigel often boasted that he made a study of people and that it had often paid off in his career and his life. This was a case in point.

'That'll be her,' said Nigel as he heaved himself out of Rafferty's low-slung settee. 'I'll let her in.'

He was soon back with a pretty girl in an all-enclosing, ankle-length mackintosh. She asked who was the groom. Nigel told her. She whipped off her mac to reveal a policewoman's uniform. She came and sat on Rafferty's knee and invited him to undo her jacket. He duly obliged and soon she was revealed to be wearing a bustier and suspenders. She turned their music off and put her own on from a CD player she'd brought with her. It played a raunchy tune that Rafferty didn't recognize.

She came to sit on his knee again and invited him to remove her stockings, which she then proceeded to drape around his neck. With a kiss, she jumped up and began the rest of her routine, bumping and grinding away to the raunchy music.

Rafferty risked a glance at Llewellyn, and was amused to see his sergeant sitting bolt upright and looking tight-faced. Llewellyn didn't approve, it was clear.

The Welshman was pretty strait-laced and not into this kind of thing at all. Well, it was too late now, he thought, as Mickey finally got the bustier undone. Rafferty sat back and enjoyed the show.

Rafferty woke and sat up, dry-mouthed and bleary-eyed. The stripper had gone. Everyone else was lounging on the furniture looking in an equally sorry state, most of them snoring. Apart from Dafyd, who still sat bolt upright. When he saw that Rafferty was awake, he said, 'We ought to think about getting your brothers home and organizing taxis for the rest.'

'Can you ring for the cabs?' Rafferty wasn't sure he'd be able to see the numbers on the phone if he tried.

Llewellyn got up and went into the hall to the phone. He

ordered cabs. When he'd done that, he started rousing every-body. This was a difficult task, but eventually, he managed to get everyone awake, if not totally compos mentis.

'I hope the cabs will take them in this condition,' said Llewellyn. 'I wouldn't, if I was the driver.'

'It's nearly five o'clock in the morning. The drivers won't be expecting entirely sober citizens. If they turn up they're prepared for this lot. Anyway, they're not fighting drunks. I'll make some coffee. It should help.'

Still under the influence of alcohol, Rafferty staggered into the kitchen. It took him five minutes to fill the kettle as it kept wavering away from the tap, but eventually, he managed to fill it. With difficulty, when the kettle boiled, he poured the water into the mugs. And all over the worktop. He found a tray and slopped the mugs on to it. He handed round the coffee he hadn't spilled on his way back from the kitchen.

It had been a good night, but he was shattered now and wanted to go to bed. He hoped the cabs didn't take long.

But the cabs arrived within another ten minutes and Nigel and the rest wove their uncertain way out into the night with loud goodbyes fit to wake the neighbours. Rafferty tried to shush them, but it was no good. They were beyond restraining.

At least they had soon stumbled their way to the taxis, which quickly drove off.

'I'll get your brothers home now,' said Llewellyn.

Mickey had gone back to sleep and Rafferty woke him up. 'Come on, bro,' he said. 'Let's be having you. I'm sure Dafyd wants to get home himself. Maureen will give me what for if he's not back soon.' Maureen was Llewellyn's wife and, like Llewellyn, wasn't a drinker. She didn't really approve of stag nights, though she had raised surprisingly few objections when Rafferty had arranged one for Llewellyn. He couldn't help but wonder what she'd think of this one, though he doubted Llewellyn would be so stupid as to mention the stripper. But Mo wasn't daft and being his cousin, knew him, Nigel and the other two Rafferty brothers as well as she knew her own.

Llewellyn quickly ushered Mickey and Patrick Sean out of the flat. Rafferty said relieved goodbyes and shut the door. He went immediately to the kitchen and drank a pint of cold water, then visited the bathroom and fell into bed. He was soon asleep. Even sooner, it seemed, it was morning and time to get up.

He groaned and sat on the side of the bed. But he didn't feel as bad as he should have. The water had helped.

He got out of bed and made for the kitchen. He was soon outside of two large mugs of tea and four aspirin. Ten minutes later, he started to feel a bit better.

He went for a shower and got dressed. He wasn't hungry, but he forced himself to eat some toast, then he made for the station. He was still hung-over and suspected he would show up as being over the limit if he was breathalysed, so he drove with wary circumspection.

Llewellyn, of course, was there before him, once again looking clear-eyed and ready for the day.

'How do you feel?' he asked Rafferty.

'Could be worse. Could be better. Let's not talk about it. I'll survive. What's come in? Anything?'

'No.'

Rafferty sighed. 'Oh, well. It's early yet. Maybe something interesting will arrive later.'

They settled down and Rafferty drank the tea Llewellyn provided every morning. He didn't do a lot of work; given the heavy night, he felt it was enough that he'd turned up. Thankfully, Superintendent Bradley didn't disturb the hung-over morning.

The day passed slowly. Rafferty rang Abra and asked her how her night had gone.

'Great,' said Abra. 'I didn't get home till five o'clock.'

'Worse than me, you dirty stop out.' But then she was twelve years younger than him and more able to take such late nights.

'How about you? Was your night good?'

'Yes. It was a terrific night, though I was glad to get to bed.'

'Your own, I hope.'

'Of course, my own. Dafyd saw to that. Not that I fancied a one-night-stand, anyway. Those days are long gone.'

'Glad to hear it.' She lowered her voice to a whisper and told him, 'I have to go, Joe, the boss is lurking. I'll see you tonight.'

'OK, sweetheart. Love you. Bye.'

'Love you.'

Rafferty put the phone down and smiled, thankful, once more, that he'd been able to remove Abra from the list of suspects and adulterers. It wasn't long now till the wedding. 'Got your glad rags sorted out for Saturday?' he asked Llewellyn.

'Yes. We're all prepared.'

Of course they were. Dafyd and Mo were an organized pair.

'What about you? Got your suit ready?'

'Yes. It's in the wardrobe waiting for the big day. I'll out bobby-dazzle even you on Saturday.'

'Just as it should be. But don't out-dazzle the bride – not a good start to a marriage.'

'No chance of that, I shouldn't think. Abra will outshine everyone, that's for sure.' He sighed and opened a file. 'We'd better try to solve this case before Saturday or there'll be a delayed honeymoon. That wouldn't be a good start to the marriage, either.'

FIFTEEN

Rafferty's investigation of the people Nigel had sent to the Staveleys' for a viewing was continuing apace. There were a surprising number of them, given the lingering effects of the recession and the cost of the house. So far, it had revealed nothing any more concrete than the rest of the investigation. Most of the viewers were able to provide an alibi for their whereabouts at the estimated time of the murder. But there were several whom Rafferty felt he needed to question himself. Two of these were couples, one of which lived in Elmhurst and the other in London. Both couples had viewed the Staveleys' house on the afternoon of the murder, as had the third viewer, a young man named Harry Bentley who also lived in Elmhurst. Or so he had said. He was the first on the list and the address he had given – 35 Dennis Street – didn't check out. There was no such address. Rafferty had thought when Nigel supplied it that the address was unfamiliar and presumed it was on one of the new estates that had sprung up in the town's surrounds.

He tackled Nigel again to find out what else he knew of the man. He went to the office rather than ring him as Nigel seemed able to be far wilier on the phone than he managed in person. Rafferty, who had attended compulsory classes in understanding body language, had retained sufficient knowledge to put some of it to the benefit of inquiries and Nigel's body often betrayed him and told Rafferty that he wasn't getting the whole truth over some given matter.

He had thought his cousin would be in a friendly frame of mind after the camaraderie of the stag night, but not a bit of it. His Jerry Kelly personality had again been subsumed into that of his estate agent alter ego and at first, he was very short and did no more than answer Rafferty's questions as briefly as he could get away with.

'Did he come into your office or phone asking for the house details?' Rafferty persisted.

'He came into the office.'

'And you're sure you gave us the right address?'

Nigel gave a careless shrug. 'I gave you the one he gave me. Not my fault if it doesn't check out.' His nose went up in the air and Rafferty noticed that his normally excessively well-groomed cousin had neglected to rid his nostrils of stray hairs. 'It's necessary to have a certain level of trust in this business, dear boy.'

Rafferty's lips thinned at Nigel's use of the 'dear' epithet. It was Nigel at his most patronising. However, he bit back his annoyance and asked, 'How did he seem, this Bentley?'

'How did he seem? Do you mean – did he have a mad glint in his eye? Because he didn't. He looked a perfectly normal, perfectly respectable, sane young man around twenty-eight or thirty. As I recall, his eyes were a rather attractive brown.'

'There's no need to be facetious. So how did you arrange the viewing? By ringing Bentley's landline or his mobile?'

'His mobile.' At last, Nigel became more expansive. 'He told me he currently lived with his mother, but that he had come into an inheritance from his grandmother. He didn't want his mother to know he was considering buying his own place, hence the use of a mobile rather than a landline. I don't suppose he wanted me to ring and leave messages with mummy. I had no reason to disbelieve him. People tell me all sorts. Some of it's even true.'

'I'll want the number.'

Nigel nodded and summoned one of his staff in a lordly manner. It was clear he didn't treat his staff in as polite a manner as he did his clients. Not for his staff the obsequious, Uriah Heep approach.

Rafferty smothered a grin. It was clear Nigel wanted to reassert his authority. Even a technophobe like him knew that such information could be stored on a computer and quickly called up. But he didn't care if he got the information from Nigel's computer or from one of his staff as long as he got it.

It looked a distinct possibility that this man, this Bentley, could be the killer. Why else give false details? Rafferty doubted the man was called Bentley, either. With a bit of luck, if he was careless, they'd be able to trace him via his mobile.

Nigel had been able to give them a pretty good description. To Rafferty's excitement, Nigel's description tallied with

the one that Edith Staveley had supplied of her attacker, at
least insofar as bodily description went, though of course the
man who had attacked Mrs Staveley had worn a balaclava.

Rafferty went back to the station and had the description
circulated. He hoped that something came from it. He also
got Llewellyn to check out Bentley's mobile.

He updated Bradley on the case and, after his very belated
confession, was torn off a strip for not finding out earlier that
the Staveley house was for sale.

'Even if they didn't have an estate agent's board outside
the property it's an easy surmise that a man who was made
redundant six months earlier might be getting short of funds
to pay the mortgage. Did you ask him?'

Given the late hour in the murder investigation in which
he had made the discovery that the Staveleys' house was for
sale, Rafferty was forced to say, 'No.'

'I thought as much. Call yourself a detective! Anyway,
you've at least managed to match him with the man who
attacked the victim's mother-in-law. I suppose that's something.'

It was clear that Bradley had forgotten Edith Staveley's
name. Not to mention that of the victim. During a previous
case, he had instigated the latest in his public relations scams.
Called 'Politeness in Interraction with Members of the Public',
he had insisted his officers behave with scrupulous politeness.
For the lower orders, it involved remembering a myriad of
names on first hearing them during an investigation. It hadn't
applied to Bradley, of course, who continued calling them
'victims'. It was so much less trouble. Rafferty had supplied
the acronym in a burst of devilment. 'PIMP' had been used
for several months before Bradley stumbled on the insubor-
dinate truth. It had amused Rafferty no end when Bradley
realized he'd been had and had been discussed with sniggers
around the station ever since. It was no wonder that he wasn't
the superintendent's favourite copper.

It turned out that Harry Bentley's number was for a pay-
as-you-go mobile – one that he seemingly didn't use very
often. Perhaps he'd bought it specially so that he would have
a number to give Nigel so he could gain access to Adrienne's
home, when all he was interested in was murder.

This raised various questions. How had Bentley known her.

Was he yet another of her lovers? But if he were, he surely
wouldn't need to go in for such elaborate plans to gain admit-
tance. He was reluctant to ask John Staveley about Bentley
in case he did turn out to be yet another of Adrienne's lovers,
but he had little choice. He had no other person to ask. But
he made sure to take Llewellyn with him when he went to
see the widower. Llewellyn was far more tactful than he ever
managed to be: he was always so eager to get on and solve
a crime that it was his habit to burst out with things that would
probably have been better left unsaid. Llewellyn was far more
studied in his remarks.

His sensitivity wasn't rewarded, however. Because, just like
before – when he'd asked Staveley about Gary Oldfield and
his wife's other men friends – the widower professed igno-
rance.

Rafferty pressed him. 'You're sure you didn't know him?
Or at least know of him?' He described Harry Bentley, but it
availed him nothing.

'No. I told you. I've never heard of the man. He must have
been another viewer that Adrienne saw on her own.'

Disgruntled, Rafferty told Staveley to ring him if he thought
of anything – either to do with this Bentley or anything else.

Later that morning, he and Llewellyn drove to London to
interview the second couple who had viewed the Staveleys'
home on the day of the murder – they would speak to the
other couple on their return.

It was a long, slow, slog into the capital. The weather had
turned foul and rain lashed the windscreen all the way along
the A12, made worse by the passing lorries, which spewed
spray up from their tyres. The trip wasn't made more bear-
able by the discovery that their journey had been a wasted
one. The couple, a Mr and Mrs Kemp, who were patrician
types in their fifties and lived in a pricey, three-storey
Kensington terrace, were able to tell them little more than
that Adrienne Staveley had been a little surly.

'It was almost as if she didn't want to sell,' Mrs Kemp told
them once they were all three seated in her surprisingly untidy
drawing room: there were books everywhere, piled on chairs,
on the floor and some of them were even stored on book-
shelves. Rafferty read a few of the titles, but they were clearly
academic tomes not meant for the layman and his eyes glazed

over. 'She certainly didn't have the demeanour of a woman keen to make a sale.'

Given that Adrienne hadn't wanted to move and was doing so only under duress this was unsurprising. Rafferty had already put the dead woman down as spoilt and selfish, so this sullen attitude was to be expected.

From the preliminary interview with the couple, conducted by Mary Carmody and Jonathon Lilley, it had been revealed that they had already known Adrienne. They had apparently met her at the dinner party of mutual friends in Chelsea – John Staveley had told them that Adrienne would often take the train to town for dinner with friends or to the theatre, though she'd always returned the same evening rather than give rise to suspicions by staying overnight. The report had inferred that the acquaintance had been more than it in fact turned out to be and both the Kemps had denied more than a passing knowledge, just a few hours' long, of the dead woman.

'She was seated at the other end of the table,' Mrs Kemp explained, 'so we barely spoke to her. It was only because she was so vivacious that we remembered her and recognized her when we went to view her home.'

'I see. Well, thank you for your time.' Rafferty was annoyed it had been such a wasted journey. Lilley and Mary Carmody would get a rocket when he got back to the station.

They took their leave of the Kemps and headed back to Elmhurst. The weather was still awful and the return journey was as bad as the outward one had been, with, seemingly, even more spray-throwing lorries on the road.

Llewellyn drove. Rafferty told him he wanted to get a bit of shut-eye, to be fresh for the afternoon. He was in with a good chance of getting forty winks as Llewellyn was a slow and steady, not to say cautious, driver, so it was unlikely that a sudden stamp on the brakes would jolt him awake.

When they finally reached Elmhurst and were able to interview the other couple, the Donaldsons, it was to find that the couple, who were staid and elderly, hadn't noticed Adrienne's vivacity and had been far more concerned with checking the agent's room measurements and pointing out faults in an attempt to get the price reduced.

They didn't say as much, of course, but it was apparent

from their every word and gesture. Sore at heart, Rafferty had had Llewellyn drive them back to the station and a late canteen lunch. It completed the day's disappointments when they found nothing but sandwiches remaining from the lunchtime repast, rather than the hot meal they had been looking forward to. The sandwiches were even salad, rather than beef or ham, much to Rafferty's even greater disappointment, though the salad perfectly suited Llewellyn.

Rafferty would have gone out to lunch, but he'd already been out all morning and nearly all of lunchtime, so he felt it prudent to show his face around the station. Besides, Bradley would surely want to know how his latest interviews had gone. Rafferty and Llewellyn weren't the only ones destined for disappointment.

When Rafferty got home that night it was to find Abra complaining about the mess the stag night boys had left behind them. 'You might have tidied up,' she told him as soon as he came through the door.

Rafferty had a vague recollection of Llewellyn trying to clear away the beer cans and other detritus, but being jeered at by the rest. Nevertheless, he had persevered and cleared a lot of the rubbish. He bit his tongue in time to stop himself revealing this fact. It wouldn't go down well if Abra learned that it had been Llewellyn rather than him, who had filled the two bulging bin bags leaning drunkenly by the kitchen door.

'I'll give you a hand,' said Rafferty. Thinking it politic to show willing, he pulled a bin bag off the strip on the table, finally got it open and started putting cans in it. 'It won't take long, then I'll ring for a home delivery meal. What do you fancy?'

'How about a Chinese?'

'Fine by me. Sweet and sour chicken OK?'

Abra nodded.

The room was soon tidied and Rafferty rang for the meal. They enjoyed a quiet evening and an early night. They both needed it and Rafferty knew he couldn't have a second day of relative idleness. Not in a murder investigation.

SIXTEEN

The following day was a busy one. But at least Rafferty didn't feel hung-over and was more able to deal with it. The team had discovered more potential witnesses and, in desperation, he and Llewellyn were out all morning questioning them. But not one of them had anything useful to confide. Indeed, several turned out to be those timewasters looking for their moment in the spotlight, which bedevilled every police inquiry. Disgruntled, they returned to the station.

Even though he'd been half-expecting it, Rafferty was even more disgruntled when he found Bradley waiting for them. The superintendent wanted an update on the investigation. He was now demanding updates twice a day, much to Rafferty's irritation. It made him even more irritated because he had no updates to give to him and didn't Bradley rub it in. If it wasn't for Bradley's desire to shine in the eyes of the bosses at Region, Rafferty would swear he was getting pleasure out of his failure.

This time, once Rafferty had provided the update, Bradley expressed himself far from satisfied. Bluntly, the superintendent told him, 'Even you can do better than this, Rafferty.' Though not much better hung in the air. 'God knows you've had long enough to sort it out. Try a bit harder. I'll be at a retirement do at HQ for most of the afternoon, but I'll want another update at the end of the day. Try to see that it's better than this one.'

Bradley left them and Rafferty met Llewellyn's eye. 'I don't know what he expects,' he complained. 'I'm doing everything I can. Aren't I?' he asked plaintively, even as he began to believe that he couldn't be or why would anyone, even Bradley, be so critical? But Llewellyn reassured him.

'I'm afraid the superintendent has been a long time out of front line policing and no longer understands the difficulties.'

'Paperwork wallah,' said Rafferty in disgust. 'That's what's wrong with the police nowadays – too many paper shufflers and not enough investigators.'

'Well, it's how things are so we have no choice but to accept it.'

Llewellyn didn't believe in expending his energy and his temper in battling against what he couldn't change.

'Yes, but we don't have to like it.'

Superintendent Bradley's unfair criticism worked as a spur and Rafferty read through the statements from scratch once again. And this time, he picked up on something he should perhaps have pursued with a bit more vigour before.

'Gary Oldfield,' he said. 'I think we should question him again. He lied to us about staying home all afternoon of the murder. I don't like liars. Not in a murder investigation, anyway,' he added as an afterthought when he recalled some of his own white lies to Abra over the honeymoon. Not to mention his silent deception over his unwarranted suspicions about her activities re the Staveleys.

'Nor do I,' said Llewellyn. 'Shall we get over there?'

Rafferty nodded and reached for his jacket.

Gary Oldfield was at work, though not with a customer this time. They found him in the lot's Portakabin, working on the computer. He must have heard them on the steps, because he turned at their entrance and the ready smile he presumably adopted for spending customers was quickly replaced by a scowl.

'Not you again,' he complained sourly. 'I'm feeling hounded.'

'Sorry about that, sir,' said Rafferty as he walked the few paces to the front of the desk and stared down at him. 'But when someone lies to us, it makes us prick up our ears.'

Oldfield scowled again. 'I told you, I forgot I went out around five that afternoon. If I'd remembered, I'd have mentioned it.'

'Even so. It wasn't very helpful. We don't like it when people are unhelpful. As I said, it makes us suspicious.'

'Yes, well. There's no need to be. I haven't done anything wrong.'

'So you say.'

Oldfield slammed the laptop shut and stood up. 'Look, I don't have to listen to this.'

Today, he was in a three-piece ensemble in dove grey. Like

all his other clothes, it looked expensive. Rafferty wondered
if Oldfield and his cousin Nigel patronized the same tailor.
'I'm afraid you do, sir. It's important that you're co-operative.
It *is* a murder investigation. Not to mention the murder investigation of your girlfriend. I thought you might actually care
that we catch her murderer.'

Oldfield sat down and gazed at Rafferty with every evidence
of sincerity. 'Of course I want you to catch her murderer, but
you've already had my co-operation. Several times. I don't
see what else I can do.'

'You can make sure you don't lie to us again,' Rafferty told
him. 'And as for having your co-operation, sometimes it takes
several conversations to get to the crux of the matter. As it
did with you.'

'Well, as you said, you've already got to the crux of the
matter in my case. I went out for a takeaway and came home
again. That's it. Full stop. Nothing more to say.'

'If we find there's nothing more to say we won't trouble
you again.'

'Good. Now, can I get on?' He glanced out of the
Portakabin's grimy window. 'I see I've got a potential customer
hovering. I might make a sale if you leave me in peace.'

Rafferty shrugged, wished him good day and walked back
to the car with Llewellyn.

'Let's question the other liar in the case,' he said, as he
tightened the seatbelt around him. 'Kyle Staveley. He should
be home from school by now.'

Kyle *was* at home and no more pleased to see them than
had been Gary Oldfield. He slammed the door behind them
after letting them in, threw himself into an easy chair and
folded his arms.

John Staveley was there and appeared no happier than his
son at their arrival. 'Was it me you wanted, Inspector?'

'No sir. It was your son we wanted to see. We need to question him again about where he went when he left the library
on the afternoon of his stepmother's murder.'

Staveley frowned and glanced at his son before turning
his attention back to Rafferty. 'I don't know how Kyle can
help you any further, Inspector. He's told you all he can
remember. Badgering him isn't going to help him recall where
he went.'

'I'm sure he *thinks* he's told us all he can. But there might be something he's remembered since we last spoke to him.'

'I don't see what. He was wandering aimlessly after he left the library, not taking any notice of where he was going.' He pulled a face. 'You could say I was doing the same and I certainly don't remember more than a few of the streets I walked down.'

'Maybe. But he lied to us about when he left the library.'

'He was scared, that's all. That's why he didn't tell you the truth. It's why he ran away to London.'

'Even so. It's still relevant to the inquiry.' He turned to the sulky-looking Kyle. 'So where was it you went when you left the library, Kyle. Have you remembered yet?'

'I just walked around, like dad says.'

'I imagine you had all your school books with you?'

'Yes.'

'Bit heavy, weren't they, for carting around?'

'I'm used to it. They don't bother me.'

'Are you sure you can't remember where you walked?'

Kyle frowned. 'I walked down the High Street.'

'Which is where the library is situated.' So it went without saying that he'd been there. 'Can you remember anywhere else?'

'I was on Bacon Lane, I remember that.'

The back entrance to the police station was on Bacon Lane – an unfortunate name given the porcine epithet that was often thrown at the police.

'What about after that? Can you remember where you went?'

Kyle was quiet for a moment, then shook his head. 'I wasn't really taking a lot of notice. I had a lot on my mind. I was thinking.'

'About what?'

'Just school stuff.'

'Not about your stepmother and your relationship?'

'No. I've always done my best not to think about her at all.'

'Was your relationship with her that bad?'

Kyle didn't answer.

John Staveley butted in. 'If there's nothing else, Inspector, Kyle's got homework to do.'

Rafferty admitted defeat for now and allowed himself to be shown out. 'Oh, well,' he said, once they were outside with the door shut firmly behind them, 'It was worth a try.'

So, where did that leave them? For the most part, with the men in the case – the Staveleys, father and son, Oldfield, Peacock and Simpson. Also, he couldn't discount Staveley's sister and brother-in-law, the Aylings. Between his lustful stalking of Adrienne and her jealousy, they provided a pretty pair of motives.

And then there was Mrs Staveley Senior, who had the bodily strength to strangle Adrienne and plenty of reasons for wanting to do so. She hadn't lied to them. She had more or less admitted that she and Adrienne hadn't seen eye to eye and she seemed the sort of woman who would act decisively to save her son from a distressing marriage and possibly even more distressing divorce. Though Rafferty found it hard to imagine her or Helen Ayling strangling Adrienne, he couldn't afford to discount them.

He mentioned his earlier thoughts to Llewellyn once they were back in the car and suggested they pay Mrs Staveley a visit. They drove out of the narrow streets of Elmhurst and after they had wound their way through the lanes, reached The White Farmhouse, where she was currently staying.

Edith Staveley was cool, but perfectly polite when she opened her son's front door. 'Inspector,' she said. 'What can I do for you?'

'Can we come in, Mrs Staveley?' he asked.

She nodded and stood back. 'I think you know where the drawing room is.'

Rafferty nodded and led the way. She invited them to sit down and did so herself. He noted that her back had now regained its former straight posture, though, perhaps, it wasn't *quite* as upright as formerly.

'I was out earlier, but my son told me you'd been here questioning Kyle again. He's only a boy. Surely you can't think he had anything to do with Adrienne's death?'

Rafferty forbore from mentioning the several cases in recent years where kids younger than Kyle had killed or seriously

injured someone, but simply told her, 'We can't discount
anyone, Mrs Staveley. Kyle's a big lad for his age and more
than capable of finding the strength required to strangle a
small woman like your late daughter-in-law.'

She was silent for several moments as she digested this.
Then she said, 'So am I, Inspector. And I had no more reason
to like Adrienne than Kyle did.'

'I know that. Did you kill her?'

Mrs Staveley hesitated a moment, then shook her head.
'No. I didn't kill her. Though if it would take suspicion off
my grandson I wish I had.'

'You said you were at home around the time your daughter-
in-law died and that nobody can confirm it, is that right?'

'Yes. Something unavoidable when one lives alone.'

'Of course. Tell me – how much did you dislike Adrienne?'

'A lot,' she told them frankly. 'I thought she was a most
unsuitable wife for my son and the worst possible stepmother
for Kyle. I wanted them to divorce even before John was
made redundant, but he wouldn't hear of it. Said the disruption would be bad for Kyle after he'd already lost his mother.'
She issued an unladylike snort. 'As if living with her wasn't
bad for Kyle. Any disruption would be welcome to get that
woman out of their lives.'

'Even the disruption that her murder has caused?'

'Yes. Even that.'

Well, thought Rafferty, at least she was honest. After all
the lies it made a refreshing change. 'Well, thank you, Mrs
Staveley,' he said as he stood up. He didn't bother to say
they'd see themselves out, remembering her insistence on
doing this herself on their first visit to her home. He
just assumed the same stricture applied in John Staveley's
house.

They drove back to the station and Llewellyn typed up the
details of their latest interviews. They didn't take him long:
he had undergone a touch-typing course some years earlier
and was the fastest typist on the team and that included the
female admin staff.

'Might as well get a very late lunch,' said Rafferty.
'Anywhere you fancy?'

'Let's try the Black Swan,' said Llewellyn to Rafferty's
surprise. He had expected the Welshman to suggest the Red

Lion, the cappuccino crowd's hangout. 'They serve meals all day,' he explained.

Rafferty nodded. 'The Black Swan it is. Come on, before Bradley waylays us.'

They set off and managed to avoid any waylaying.

SEVENTEEN

When they got to the Black Swan Rafferty ordered mushroom omelette and chips and Llewellyn had a mixed salad with jacket potato.

The food soon arrived and they tucked in. Rafferty's omelette was beautifully fluffy with plenty of mushrooms, and he gave it his full attention as such good food deserved.

Llewellyn's salad came with French bread and he seemed to be enjoying his meal every bit as much – he certainly didn't seem inclined to talk, either. With their undivided attention, the meals were soon devoured. As the plates were removed, they thanked the waitress and sipped their drinks.

'Any ideas as to where we should go on this case?' Rafferty asked as he put his Adnams Bitter down. It was a question he was aware he was asking too often. He was the senior investigating officer on the case – the ideas were meant to come from him. He should be conducting the investigation and leading the team, not expecting the answers to come from his subordinates.

Llewellyn sipped his mineral water. 'None. We seem to be stalemated and unless something breaks . . .'

'Unless something breaks – when have I heard that before?'

'On every case we've conducted, it seems and we – you – always got the answer in the end.'

'I did, didn't I?' Pensively, Rafferty took another sip of his beer. 'But this might just turn out to be the case where I fail.'

'It's not like you to be so defeatist.'

'Normally, I've got somewhere to go, but on this one, we've already been over the statements twice more, with precious little to show for our efforts. We've questioned the suspects till I can think of nothing else to ask them.'

'I know.' Llewellyn finished his mineral water. 'Perhaps we should get back.'

'I suppose so.' Reluctantly, Rafferty downed the rest of his beer and got to his feet. 'Come on, then.'

There was nothing of any interest awaiting them on their

return – not even Superintendent Bradley. The idle sod was presumably still chucking back the booze at the retirement do. Maybe it would make him forget to get a further update on his return.

Rafferty glanced desultorily through the earlier statements, but nothing leapt out at him. He hadn't expected it to. Not really. He realized he was clutching at straws. He glanced at the clock on the wall. It was nearly five o'clock. They were achieving nothing here, so he suggested they have an early night. And at least it would enable him to escape a boozed up and probably belligerent Bradley – though he wasn't sure that being questioned by the hung-over version wouldn't be infinitely worse.

The wedding was getting nearer with no solution to the murder in sight. It was beginning to look as if cancelling the honeymoon was inevitable. It was such a shame. He'd leave it as late as possible, but he didn't hold out much hope of a last-minute miracle.

They headed out to the car park together and went their separate ways.

Abra was surprised to see him home so early and for a moment she looked hopeful. 'Don't tell me you've solved the case?'

'No such luck, I'm afraid.' He took the bull by the horns with a vigour not matched by the best of matadors. 'I think we really may have to cancel the honeymoon, sweetheart.'

Abra took it surprisingly well. 'I feared as much. Never mind, we can go later in the year as we'll get the cancellation insurance.'

'Yes,' Rafferty fibbed. He still hadn't told Abra that they *had* no insurance. He'd just have to raid what little remained of his savings to pay for another honeymoon.

They had a scratch meal as they'd both had a late lunch and weren't very hungry. Abra quizzed him some more on the murder investigation, but there was little enough to tell. The case was stalemated as Llewellyn had said and no amount of talking would make any difference.

They sat down on the settee with a bottle of Jameson's between them and enjoyed a few nightcaps. As he drank, Rafferty was reminded of Superintendent Bradley and he grimaced at the thought of facing him in the morning. A similar thought seemed to strike Abra, for she asked, 'How's Superintendent Bradley taking your failure to solve the case?'

'Like it's a personal affront. Like I'm doing it deliberately just to spite him. Stupid man. Let's not talk about him.'

'OK. What do you want to talk about?'

'The wedding and our lives together. I want Saturday to be a happy day for both of us.'

'It will be. You realize I'll be going to stay at my flat the night before the wedding?'

'Yes. It's traditional that we shouldn't see each other. We don't want to invite bad luck,' said the ever superstitious Rafferty. 'I'll miss you.'

'It's only for one night. You'll survive.'

'I suppose so, Still, the flat will be empty without you.'

'All the more reason to appreciate me while I *am* here.'

'I appreciate you, Abracadabra, don't ever think I don't. You know I love you to bits.'

'Ditto. Shall we go to bed? It seems to have been a long day one way and another.'

'My day's been a bit like that, too. Yes. Let's go to bed. I could do with a good night's sleep.'

'I wasn't thinking of sleeping,' Abra told him.

It was two days before the wedding and Rafferty was losing hope about the case and the honeymoon. But then something broke that gave him renewed reason to think that, after all, they might yet crack the case and get away.

Another witness had come forward to state that they had seen Gary Oldfield near the Staveleys' house around five thirty-five on the evening of the murder.

Rafferty was exuberant. 'He lied to us again. How come his car didn't show up?' He slapped the desk and answered his own question. 'Stupid of me – he had a whole yard full of vehicles to choose from. He could easily have walked from his flat to the car lot wearing a hoodie so the CCTV cameras couldn't show up his features. He had the keys to the key cabinet, so could take whatever car he fancied so his own didn't show up on CCTV.'

'It seems likely,' said Llewellyn.

'It's more than likely. Crafty sod. This witness should help us nail him. Let's get over there and bring him in.'

'Don't you think it might be a good idea first to send an officer to the used car lot to make a note of all the registration numbers and then to see if one matches up to the CCTV footage near the Staveley's home?'

'You're right, of course. It'll strengthen our arm when we question him again.'

But before they could get this organized, one of the team came in with the news that Harry Bentley had used his mobile at last. They'd traced him to a house on Danes Road.

'Danes Road?' Rafferty repeated. 'Not number 35, by any chance?'

'Yes, sir,' said a bewildered Constable Gerry Hanks. 'How did you know that?'

'Never mind. It doesn't matter.' Bloody Nigel. Called himself an estate agent and he couldn't even take down an address properly.

It was several hours later by the time they'd sorted through the relevant CCTV tapes to see if Gary Oldfield had used one of the car lot's vehicles.

Rafferty's eyes felt as bleary as on the morning after his stag do after staring at the screen so long. But this was something he wanted to check for himself. It turned out to be a well-earned bleariness – he'd caught one of the cars from the used car lot. Llewellyn had been right. It had been a good idea to wait and get the second piece of evidence against Oldfield.

They hurried out to the car park and drove to Oldfield's place of work.

He was there, large as life and twice as sure of himself. As though to exhibit how little concern he felt for their latest visit, he ran careless fingers through his springy, dark brown curls. It irritated Rafferty as much now as it had the first time he'd met him.

'This really is becoming a bad habit, Inspector. So what can I do for you this time?' he asked.

'It's more a case of what I can do for you,' Rafferty told him. 'I can arrest you for the murder of Adrienne Staveley.' He gave the shocked and no longer so cocky Oldfield the statutory caution and escorted him to the car.

The circumstantial evidence against Oldfield was stacking up. He'd lied to them not once, not twice, but three times.

He'd been having an affair with Adrienne, who had started to become demanding. And he had stood to lose his girlfriend if Adrienne had taken the natural next step to break the couple up by telling Diana Rexton about the affair. He couldn't be sure that his girlfriend would accept his infidelity. For all he knew Diana Rexton would leave him and take his dreams of wealth with her.

All those taken together built up a pretty solid case. But it didn't move Oldfield, who continued to deny that he'd killed Adrienne. He even denied taking one of the cars from the lot, which was a pointless denial as the car had been captured on CCTV. 'I left the flat once around the time of the murder,' he continued to insist, 'and that's all. Whoever's told you different is a liar with an axe to grind.'

'One of your customers, perhaps,' Rafferty said. 'I've heard there have been one or two with reasons for complaint.'

Oldfield looked torn between agreeing with this statement or denying that his customers had anything to complain about.

'I didn't do it,' he insisted mulishly, when they questioned him again after seeing if a spell in the cells would work its occasional magic. 'OK, I admit that Adrienne was pushing for us to live together. That was never going to happen, as I told her. I didn't want to lose Diana. I love her.'

'Love her money, more like,' said Rafferty.

'I know she has money. What do you think I am, stupid? Why do you think I joined the tennis club, but to hook myself a rich bird? Most were stuck-up bitches, too pretty and spoilt to be worth my while. But Diana is plain and homely, I thought she'd be grateful for my attentions and she was. She still is.' He grinned, not at all abashed by his sojourn in the cells.

'Come on, Gary,' he said. 'You were scared that in order to push you into doing what she wanted she would tell Diana about your affair. Why won't you admit it?'

'Because it isn't true. Even if Adrienne *had* told Diana of our affair, she'd have forgiven me. She's a very forgiving sort, Diana, as is proved by the fact that she *did* know of my affair and only left me for a day or two. Anyway, this is all very interesting, but not very accurate. I didn't kill her. I didn't have time, as you'd realize if you weren't so keen on fitting me up. And, for what I hope will be the final time, for the record, I deny that I was out, driving one of my boss's cars around five thirty. I was back at the flat with Diana long before that.'

'Unfortunately, your girlfriend says she was in the bath having a long soak. You could have slipped out and gone anywhere.'

'Well I didn't and you can't prove that I did. You say you've got a witness. Well, he's wrong. And if that's all the evidence you've got, it's his word against mine.'

'Maybe. Maybe not. But I mightn't need his evidence. With the right jury I'll get a conviction on the circumstantial evidence alone.'

But stubbornly, Oldfield still continued to repeat his innocence and Rafferty knew he had no choice but to leave it to the courts. He had a strong case and with the right judge who gave the desired direction to the jury, he'd win his case. But maybe he wouldn't have to. Maybe, between now and the trial Oldfield would decide on a guilty plea. Especially if they dropped the case to manslaughter.

But murder or manslaughter, he was going away.

Rafferty thought it likely that if he did decide to plead guilty, Oldfield would claim that the murder had been an accident, an unpremeditated affair. Though if that were the case, it didn't explain why Oldfield had felt it necessary to drive a car other than his own to see Adrienne.

Rafferty felt a quiet satisfaction. He also felt relieved because he could now go on honeymoon with a clear conscience. He couldn't wait to ring Abra and tell her.

EIGHTEEN

Rafferty was eager to ring Abra and let her know that the honeymoon was back on. But first he wanted to get Oldfield's statement typed up. This was one he didn't mind doing himself. And after that, he'd again question Oldfield about his decision to use one of the cars from the used car lot when he'd visited Adrienne.

If the visit had been as innocent of evil intentions as he'd tried to convince them, why had he felt the need to do this? He supposed he'd tell them some cock and bull story about his car not starting. It might get the charge down to manslaughter. But murder or manslaughter, Oldfield was going away. And now, so were Rafferty and Abra. His destination – prison. Theirs, the south of France.

Diana Rexton was in reception when he went down. He knew Oldfield had rung her, presumably to ask her to get a hotshot lawyer to get him out from under.

He went up to her and told her she might as well go home. Gary wouldn't be leaving apart from when he made his trip to the local Magistrates' Court in the morning.

'Can I see him?' she asked.

'I'm afraid not. We've settled him down for the night. He can't see anyone but his brief.'

'I see. Even so, I think I'll stay. I feel closer to him here. He didn't do it, you know. You'll find out soon and have to let him go.'

Rafferty shrugged and left her to her lonely vigil. He took his car keys from his pocket, went out to the car park and drove home.

Abra was jubilant and they danced around the living room, so pleased the honeymoon was back on and nothing had to be cancelled.

It was late and he wanted to take her out to dinner to celebrate, but he didn't think he'd find anywhere prepared to feed them; most restaurants wouldn't take orders after nine o'clock. Then he remembered the Italian restaurant they had gone to when he asked her to marry him. The owner, a mock Italian called Senor Fabio, but really Fred Ollins from Ongar, might let them in and feed them. With a suitable bribe. He quickly checked the number in the yellow pages and rang him, ready to plead. But it wasn't necessary. It was midweek and he was presumably glad of the custom.

They didn't even bother getting changed, but just went out as they were, to save time.

It was a tipsy evening, full of reminiscences and Abra's compliments on the fact that Rafferty had solved the murder at the eleventh hour.

'Who's a clever policeman, then?' she asked sloppily, drunk on Chardonnay and happiness.

'I am,' said Rafferty, full of Jameson's and victory and the secret pleasure that, whether she liked it or not, he had saved Diana Rexton from the avaricious Oldfield.

They didn't bother with a taxi, but walked home, hand in hand, and talked of their dreams for the future, their hoped-for new home and their wedding day. After making love, they fell asleep in each other's arms.

Rafferty jerked up from his pillows and stared into the dark bedroom. God, he'd had such a vivid dream. It was about the investigation and he'd dreamt that he'd put an innocent person away. Gary Oldfield! Innocent! he scoffed to himself.

He checked the clock radio. It was three in the morning. He groaned. Not again. His head throbbed and he felt a bit queasy. He hoped he wasn't coming down with something. He thought he'd had enough alcohol to keep him safely in the arms of Morpheus for the entire night, but now he was wide awake. Worse, he had a niggle. A niggle of doubt about Oldfield's guilt. It was a niggle he didn't want and he tried to force it from his mind. But it wouldn't go away. It wasn't just a dream, then.

Something wasn't right. Oldfield had continued to deny any guilt in the murder. The trouble was, he was starting to believe him. But surely it couldn't be true? There was too much coincidental evidence stacked against him. Everything pointed to him. The car was a vehicle from his car lot. He had the only keys to open the key cabinet. He was Adrienne's lover and she'd been pressing him to set up home with her which was the last thing Oldfield would want with his little rich girl girl-friend whom he had expectations of marrying.

But a Vauxhall Vectra. Would Oldfield really choose to drive such a car when he had a whole yard full of vehicles? All right, he'd want to keep a low profile if he was going out with murder on his mind, but Rafferty thought that, given the nature of the man, he would still choose a car with a bit more oomph to it. His own car was an old-style Jaguar.

There must be a logical explanation for the way he was feeling; he'd felt this way before and it had never let him down.

He leant back against his pillows and listened to the soft breathing of Abra lying beside him. Gary Oldfield was guilty as hell. Why he'd – Rafferty stopped mid-thought, shocked as he recalled something disturbing that destroyed his confident conclusion to the case. It was something that had been said to him. But what was it? Even now his dream was fading and he cudgelled his brain as he tried to recapture its essence. He closed his eyes and shut out everything but his thoughts. He drifted and let his mind wander.

But that couldn't be right, he thought as he sat up again. Oldfield's the killer. Everything points to him. All the evidence says so.

It was then that he remembered Llewellyn and his frequent advice not to run ahead of the evidence. Was that what he'd done here? He'd been so obsessed with getting a case against Oldfield that he now realized he'd given too little thought to another person who had ample reason to murder Adrienne. He thought it through. How on earth had he missed it? How had Llewellyn missed it? Rafferty shook his head, wondering if his certainty partway through the investigation had succeeded in blinding Llewellyn also.

He could lie there no longer; his restless mind was making his body restless also and would wake Abra. He climbed out of bed and went along to the kitchen to make tea. He brought it into the living room. He sipped and thought, sipped and thought. And finally, he had it. It made sense. Everything made sense, even the choice of car.

He would have to go back to the station. He'd had too much to drink to drive. And instead of ringing for a taxi he decided to walk. He walked to the front door, pulled it open and stuck his head out and sniffed. It was a nice night, soft and balmy, with the merest hint of dampness in the air. If he was right he'd be back long before Abra woke.

He came back into the bedroom and got dressed in the clothes he'd discarded so hastily hours earlier. He needed to get to the station. The proof he required was there.

Rafferty went into reception. Diana Rexton was still there. She had been crying, he saw. Her eyes and nose were red and made her plain face plainer than ever.

The sight of her made him feel guilty and he hurried past her and through the security door.

He watched the CCTV footage for the second time and had his suspicions confirmed. Before, he had been so concentrated on finding the right registration number amongst the myriad of vehicles on the roads around the Staveleys' house during the two-hour period that Sam Dally had said the murder had taken place, that when he had found it he had seized on it and looked no further. But this time he did. And he saw what he expected to see.

Diana Rexton looked up when he appeared and said, 'Inspector Rafferty. I've been waiting for you.'

He walked up to her and said, 'It was you, wasn't it? It was you who killed Adrienne Staveley. It has to be. You weren't in the bath at all, were you? No wonder I believed you when you said Oldfield was at the flat all afternoon and evening. You were telling the truth. It shone from you. You really thought he was there and he was, apart from when he popped out for a takeaway. But you weren't. When did you take his keys? That evening? Or did you steal them earlier in the week and get copies made?'

Diana Rexton said nothing. Rafferty gave her the official caution and led her through to the charge room. Once he'd done that and seen her shut away in a cell, he went back to his office and rang Llewellyn, sure he'd want to be in at the finish as he'd been in at the beginning.

'You went to see Adrienne Staveley, didn't you? Why don't you tell us about it?'

Beside him, Llewellyn shifted in his chair, but Rafferty was concentrated on what he was saying and it didn't put him off his pursuit of the truth.

'You're right,' she told him. 'Since Gary's been locked up, I've realized I had to tell you the truth. I couldn't leave him languishing in a cell. I love him too much for that. I did go to see Adrienne Staveley. As you know, I had discovered Gary had been seeing her. And although I didn't want to ask Gary about it, I decided to speak to her. It took me a while to pluck up the nerve to challenge her. Hateful woman. I don't know what Gary saw in her.'

She probably didn't at that, thought Rafferty. He certainly couldn't imagine her making such explicit entries in her diary as those that Adrienne had made.

'What did she say?'

'She boasted of the affair as soon as she knew who I was. Said she'd made a play for him and he'd been more than willing. Said I'd been lucky to have Gary to myself for so long. So long! I only moved in with him two months ago.'

'And what did you say to her?'

'I'm afraid I wasn't very polite. I'm ashamed that I sank to her level and began name-calling. I told her that she was a promiscuous bitch and the only reason I'd be lucky was if, through Gary, she hadn't given me a sexual disease.'

'I don't suppose that went down too well.'

'No.' Diana gave a faint smile, then the smile faltered and her lips tightened. 'She called me a naive little rich girl and told me Gary was only with me for my money. He isn't. It's not true. He didn't know I had money when he pursued me at the tennis club. Nor when he asked me out. She told me that if I couldn't keep my boyfriend to heel I couldn't be much of a woman. I've never thought of myself as much of a woman,' she admitted. 'That's why I couldn't believe it when Gary kept seeking me out at the tennis club. Nor when he asked me out.

'Anyway, there was a bit more name-calling on both sides, but it was clear there wasn't a lot else to say. She was shameless. I decided to retain my dignity and walk away.'

Poor bitch, was Rafferty's thought. 'And what time did you leave Mrs Staveley?'

'I wasn't there long. I left about five fifteen. I could see I wasn't going to be able to appeal to her better nature. It was clear she didn't have one.'

'How did you know where she lived?'

'The friend I told you about – the one who followed them when they left the pub that day – she followed them to her home, so I knew where to find her.'

'How long ago did you find out about their affair?'

'Around three weeks ago.'

'And yet you said nothing to Mr Oldfield?'

'No. I wanted to make sure of the facts for myself before I confronted him.'

Rafferty suspected she would never have confronted Oldfield, scared in case he dumped her. In his estimation, she was probably safe from that. It was her money that was the attraction and he couldn't see Oldfield willingly waving goodbye to that.

'Where did you go? Back home?'

She shook her head. 'No. I just drove round for a while. After seeing that bitch and getting her confirmation that my friend was right and that she was having an affair with Gary I didn't want to go home and confront him. Not just then. I needed to get my head around the fact of his affair before I saw him again. I wanted to think what I was going to do.'

'What made you go back?'

'I was in the car and the radio was on. The DJ played that song by Dolly Parton. You know the one? Jolene. I felt the same as the girl in the song. She begged Jolene not to take her man. That was how I felt. I was scared she'd take Gary from me. She had everything that I didn't – she was attractive, vivacious, sure of herself and her femininity. I know I'm plain and dumpy and if she truly wanted to take him away from me, she could. I went back to ask her intentions. She was even more nasty than the first time I spoke to her.'

Diana Rexton looked distraught. 'She laughed at me. She was vile. Said some horrible things to me. And when she told me she meant to get Gary to set up home with her all the rejections of my teen years flashed past my eyes and I just saw red. I put my hands round her neck and squeezed. She wasn't having Gary. That was all I thought. She wasn't having Gary. If she hadn't laughed at me. If she hadn't said she would take Gary from me, she might still be alive.'

EPILOGUE

The morning of Rafferty and Abra's wedding finally dawned. It was a beautifully clear day, with an azure sky and a light breeze to keep the air fresh.

Llewellyn was round the flat early already dressed in his wedding suit. He chivvied Rafferty into getting showered and having some breakfast.

'You're like an old mother hen,' Rafferty complained. 'There's plenty of time.'

'Someone's got to make sure the day goes smoothly and as I'm best man, that's my job.'

'I suppose so. You're doing a good job so far. Better keep it up. Abra will be upset if anything goes wrong.'

'I know. And she'll blame me.'

'I doubt it. She's more likely to blame me.'

'Well, let's make sure there's no blame to be attached to either of us,' said Llewellyn. 'I think you should shower and get into your wedding suit now. We don't want to be late.'

'Yes, sir.' Rafferty went off to the bathroom, wiping toast crumbs from his mouth on the way.

The phone rang while he was in there and, worried that it was Abra telling him the wedding was off, he hurried through his ablutions and, half-dried, he hurried back to the living room. 'Who was on the phone?'

'It was Bill Beard at the station.'

'Oh. Panic over,' he said, 'Nice of him to ring with good wishes.'

'He didn't ring for that. He rang to let us know that the man who attacked and tried to strangle Edith Staveley has been caught after he forced his way into another woman's home. He's in the cells now.'

'Who caught him?'

'Timothy Smales.'

Rafferty was amazed. 'Not wet-behind-the-ears Timmy?' Rafferty laughed. 'Well, well done him. I suppose he'll come in for Mrs Staveley's reward money. He could have taken us all out for a drink. Shame I'll be on my honeymoon and not able to take advantage of his generosity. Still, not a bad haul, Daff – two criminals caught for the price of one. Diana Rexton must really love Oldfield to have strangled Adrienne when she threatened to take Gary away from her. All that passion spent on such a rat. She must have been mad.'

'As Horace says in his *Epistles:* "*Ira furor brevis est.*" Anger is a brief madness. He goes on to say we should control our passions lest they control us.'

'He's not wrong, old Horace. What a wiseacre.'

Time hung heavy after he'd got dressed in his wedding finery, but finally it was time to leave for St Boniface Church. Dafyd drove them so they were in plenty of time.

Rafferty got the fidgets once seated in the front pew. He kept looking at his watch and checking behind him. He half-feared that Abra wouldn't turn up, even though he'd spoken to her several times that morning just to reassure himself. His ma tapped him on the shoulder and told him to keep still.

Rafferty tutted and turned back to face the altar. At last, the organist struck up with the wedding march and he turned to watch Abra walk up the aisle on her father's arm.

He got up from his seat and stood before the altar to wait for her to reach him. He gave her a quick smile and Father Kelly launched into the wedding service.

This time Rafferty's mind didn't wander and he made his responses promptly.

The service was over surprisingly quickly. He and Abra went off to sign the register. They came back to smiles and a few cheers. Rafferty was grinning from ear to ear. He gave Abra another kiss when they got outside.

The photographer took some time to get them organized, but eventually he managed it. 'Now let's have the bride and groom,' he said.

Everyone else wandered off and left Rafferty and Abra alone on the church steps.

'Hello, Mrs Rafferty,' he said. 'Got you at last.'

'Or it could be said that I've got *you*,' she told him with a smile.

'True. Let's say we've got each other and leave it at that.'

Next, the photographer asked for the bride, groom and parents. After a lot more takes, and with plenty of advice from

Kitty Rafferty, the photographer was satisfied and allowed them to walk across to the church hall.

With the ordeal of the ceremony behind him, Rafferty was keen to get stuck into the booze – it would help sustain him for the speech.

Father Kelly was there ahead of them to welcome them. 'So you've finally done it, Joseph,' he remarked as he and Abra entered the beautifully decorated church hall.

'Yes,' Rafferty replied. 'It's the happiest day of my life.'

'It's glad for you I am. And the weather's been with you. God must be smiling on your union.'

'I hope so. Are you staying for the reception, Father?'

'Sure I am. I've nothing on for the rest of the day. I made certain of it. I wet your head at your baptism, isn't it only right that I wet another part of your anatomy at your wedding? Especially as this one's a much happier event than your last marriage ever was.'

There was no gainsaying this, so Rafferty didn't bother trying. 'Well, enjoy yourself,' he told the priest.

'Oh, I'll do that right enough. I aim to get your ma on the floor later.'

Rafferty laughed and he and Abra headed for the top table. His ma and Llewellyn were already there.

'Have you got your speech?' his ma asked, still acting as if she were the only woman in his life; certainly the only one with the sense to check.

'Yes.' Rafferty patted his top pocket. Llewellyn had made sure of it before they had left the flat. Sometimes, he felt like he had two mothers checking up on him and keeping him on the straight and narrow. That his ma, the buyer of stolen goods, should think to do this would be amusing if it wasn't so annoying.

'Well—' he turned to Abra – 'how does it feel to be Mrs Rafferty?'

'Strange. Ask me again in a few weeks.'

Everyone else found their seats and the caterers began to serve the meal: chicken and rice. The servings were small and Rafferty eyed his new wife's plate.

'This is tasty,' he said. 'Are you sure you want all of yours, Abra?'

'Yes, I'm sure, greedy-guts. Eat your own and take your eyes off my plate.'

After the meal it was time for the speeches. Rafferty took a gulp of wine, stood up and fingered his tie. It seemed to be choking him. 'Ladies and gentlemen,' he began. To his surprise, his speech, though short, was well received. But not as well received as Llewellyn's, which was witty and rather longer than Rafferty's effort. He even cracked a joke or two at Rafferty's expense.

But at last, all the speechifying was over and he could relax and enjoy himself. The band appeared on the stage and launched into *A Little Loving*.

'They're playing our song,' he told Abra with a wry smile. 'Let's get the dancing started.'

Soon, other couples joined them on the dance floor and the evening began to go with a swing.

True to his word, Father Kelly had Rafferty's ma up on the dance floor and waltzed her around the room with an expert's flourish. Rafferty wondered where he'd learned to dance so well. Sure sign of a youth as misspent as the rest of his life, he thought.

It didn't take long for nearly everyone to get up. Soon the room was heaving and it became hot with so many gyrating bodies. Rafferty pulled Abra off the floor to get some more liquid refreshment.

'By the way,' he said as they were waiting for the drinks to be served, 'did I tell you you look gorgeous?'

'No. Do I? Thank you.'

'No. Thank you for agreeing to become my wife. I never thought I'd see this day. It's been such a long wait.'

'The best things are worth waiting for, Joseph Aloysius. Did your mammy never tell you that?'

'Not that name again. Are you going to torture me with it for the rest of our married life?'

'Very probably.'